The FINE ART
of MURDER

Center Point
Large Print

**This Large Print Book carries the
Seal of Approval of N.A.V.H.**

The FINE ART of MURDER

A Katherine Sullivan Mystery

EMILY BARNES

CENTER POINT LARGE PRINT
THORNDIKE, MAINE

This Center Point Large Print edition is published in
the year 2016 by arrangement with Crooked Lane Books,
an imprint of The Quick Brown Fox & Company, LLC.

The text of this Large Print edition is unabridged.
In other aspects, this book may vary
from the original edition.
Printed in the United States of America
on permanent paper.
Set in 16-point Times New Roman type.

ISBN: 978-1-68324-007-5

Library of Congress Cataloging-in-Publication Data

Names: Barnes, Emily (Mystery author), author.
Title: The fine art of murder : a Katherine Sullivan mystery / Emily
Barnes.
Description: Center Point Large Print edition. | Thorndike, Maine :
Center Point Large Print, [2016]
Identifiers: LCCN 2016010181 | ISBN 9781683240075
    (hardcover : alk. paper)
Subjects: LCSH: Ex-police officers—Fiction. | Family secrets—Fiction.
| Large type books. | GSAFD: Mystery fiction.
Classification: LCC PS3602.A77563655 F56 2016 | DDC 813/.6—dc23
LC record available at https://lccn.loc.gov/2016010181

Chapter One

They say that 85 percent of those who travel return to the same place again and again. And I had to wonder, do people really play it that safe? Are there no adventurous souls out there? But then I realized that maybe the place those people are always returning to is home . . .

It had been a long, arduous day working my way from Taos to Minneapolis. With all the regulations, delays, connecting flights, and that garlic pizza the man beside me was wolfing down, I was beginning to feel I would have been better off walking. Flying used to be fun "back in the olden days," as my granddaughter referred to any time before she was born. Now it was like being packed into one of those little cars at the circus. When it stops in the middle of the ring, a dozen animated bodies come flying out, and you wonder how they all fit inside that tiny vehicle. And where was I when it became too much work to put on actual clothes? Everyone dresses so casually for a trip. The girl across from me was wearing purple and yellow pajamas. Now that's going a bit too far. I used to buy a new outfit for a flight. Maybe that was going too far the other way.

The 747 circled the Minneapolis–St. Paul

airport, for a third time, and in spite of my exhaustion, I had to admit it was a miracle. Just a few hours ago, I had been looking down at the mountainous landscape of the Southwest, everything covered in dusty sages and purples. And now the earth below me was suddenly covered in bright greens and watery blues. The mountains had slowly shrunk as we flew east, transforming themselves into soft, rolling hills.

It had been six months since I'd been home. Sully and I hadn't traveled much in our younger years. That was something for later, to be enjoyed after retirement. Each day's worth of mail always brought in two or three brochures featuring destinations we'd discuss. At the top of his list was Italy—Tuscany in particular. Paris headed mine. Even though he could have retired years before, my husband kept adding on another year in the police force, trying to up his pension so we could travel first class. But when he was shot in the line of duty, I was left alone with our plans . . . and piles of pamphlets. Even after he'd been gone a year, those colorful, glossy booklets kept coming. It was like he was telling me to hit the road and make those journeys for the both of us. So I retired early, sold the house, and packed my bags.

"Mother!"

Lizzie got out of her car and ran toward me. My heart filled with love at the sight of her.

I held my arms open. When she hugged me, it was as if she was holding on for dear life. She was my baby girl even if the calendar said she was thirty-eight.

"I'm so glad you're here. Six months is way too long."

"I agree, sweetheart." After a motherly moment, I held her at arm's length. "Your hair's so much longer. It's not as—"

"Severe?"

"No, Lizzie, nothing about you has ever been severe. I was going to say 'serious,' which is a good thing when you're a pretty blonde. You don't want to be typecast, do you? Didn't want people making blonde jokes when you were a defense attorney. It's just that now you look softer . . . and happy."

"I am—most of the time. But this divorce has been so hard. Thanks for coming."

"I'll always come when you need me." I squeezed her tight and kissed her cheek. I had to keep a brave face in spite of the fact that I was concerned about the possibility of a custody battle.

A warm breeze rippled the red silk scarf around her neck. "How long are you planning on staying?" she asked me.

"No appointments to keep anymore; I'm all yours."

"Yeah, you say that now, but after a few weeks, you get that look in your eyes. You have terminal wanderlust, Mother."

"I never thought you noticed."

An airport guard approached, waving his arms. "Move on ladies. Pick up and drive on. This is not a parking lot." He started to walk away, then stopped, spun around, and came back to us. "Hey, Chief! Is that you?"

I looked up at the tall man in the orange vest. "Stanley Nelson. It's been a while. How are you?"

"Great, Chief. I retired about a year after you did. Let the kids chase the bad guys for a while. My wife and I just celebrated our thirty-fifth anniversary."

"That's wonderful. Congratulations. But why aren't you off enjoying that retirement?" I asked him.

"A man can only fish for so long. I had to find something better to do with my time. So I got on here part time."

"What about grandchildren?" I asked.

"Five, can you believe it? And let's see . . . yours must be teenagers now?"

I nodded. "Chloe and Cameron are thirteen and fourteen."

"Good luck with that! Kids sure ain't the same as when ours were that age. It's a crazy time we're living in."

Lizzie stood at my side and I suddenly felt rude. "You remember my daughter, Elizabeth, don't you, Stan?"

"I sure do." He smiled and shook Lizzie's hand.

"Last I heard, you were a big-time attorney. Your mama was always so proud of you. And your dad, too. He was a great guy."

"Yeah, he was," Lizzie said.

"I remember you stopping by the station when you were in high school. Always with your nose stuck in some fat book."

A shuttle-bus driver honked his horn, and when I looked behind me, I saw a line of cars backed up along the curb.

"Sorry, Chief, but I have to get back to work and ask you to move your car. It was real nice seeing you again. You look great—even out of uniform."

"You, too, Stanley," I said as he walked away.

Lizzie opened the trunk, and we loaded my suitcase and paint box into her car.

She walked around to get into the driver's seat while I settled in next to her. After we fastened our seat belts, Lizzie pulled out of the Minneapolis–St. Paul airport and headed east on 62 to Edina.

Edina, Minnesota, located southwest of Minneapolis, was established in the 1860s to accommodate farms and mills. It was nothing but patchwork fields and rolling hills when I was a kid, but time passes and everything changes. Now the population is fifty thousand plus and Edina is considered one of the most affluent areas in the state. Besides being featured in several black comedies produced by the Coen brothers of *Fargo* fame, it has some of the country's best schools, fifteen parks, two country clubs, twenty-two churches—but only two hotels. The reason for the lack of lodging dates all the way back to the 1930s when the town was "dry." I guess some things change at a slower rate than others.

"Now if you would have asked me to visit in the winter," I told Lizzie, "that would have been a whole different ball game. But spring— Minnesota's version of it anyway—that's doable."

"You know," she said, unlocking the front door, "from the way you talk, it sounds as if you live in Florida or California—"

"With all the other senior citizens? Sorry, honey, but just because I don't want to deal with below zero temperatures, frozen pipes, ice, and snow does not mean I'm old. No . . . I'm sensible."

"Get off it, Mother, you've lived here your whole life. And you're not old."

With my tote bag in one hand, I grabbed the handle of the large suitcase with the other and pulled it behind me as I walked into the house. Lizzie picked up my paint box and followed.

"Well, that was then . . . now I'm just a visitor in a strange land."

Closing the front door, Lizzie said, "Follow me, stranger. Let's get you settled in the guestroom and I'll make us some lunch."

The bedroom was lovely, decorated in pastel, calming colors. As I unbuttoned my jacket, I admired the lampshade on the small dresser. It was covered with hundreds of buttons, some round, some square, most of them ivory, with a few lilac and yellow ones scattered in. "This is new, isn't it?"

"Yes, I got it last week at a fundraiser for the homeless shelter in town. I had to have it."

"I can see why." I started to open my suitcase but she stopped me.

"You must be starved. When was the last time you ate?"

"Early this morning, in Taos. I had the best green chili omelet at a little café outside of town. The sun was just coming up . . . but now that you mention it, I am hungry."

"Well tonight you can watch the sunset while you dine on steak and potatoes out on the deck."

"Perfect." I put my arm around her as we walked from the bedroom to the kitchen. "When will the kids be home? I have presents."

"In about two hours. That gives us plenty of time to catch up." She opened the refrigerator while I sat myself down at the table. "How about a tuna fish sandwich? I got that bread you like from the bakery by the park."

"Sounds good. Is there anything I can do?" I asked, hoping she'd refuse my offer. It felt so good to just relax.

Chapter Two

Between bites of sandwiches and sips of iced tea, we talked about Lizzie's divorce. She hadn't actually said it was the main reason she wanted me to visit, but I knew my daughter. As I calmly nodded and listened, I kept reminding myself that the man she was so upset with would forever be the father of my grandchildren. I sympathized, assuring her that the anger gripping her would turn to accep-tance . . . eventually. And once that happened, she might even feel friendly toward Tom.

But the truth was that I never liked Thomas Farina. Sully used to joke that it wasn't Lizzie's fault she fell for him. "He has an actor's good looks and a maître d's charm," he'd say. "What's not to like?"

Most mothers would have been thrilled to have their only daughter marry one of the most successful surgeons in the Twin Cities area. Their wedding was spectacular; they honey-mooned in Spain. But with Lizzie's demanding schedule at the law firm and his at the hospital, I knew a large portion of her life would consist of too many lonely nights and cancelled vacations. And while that adventurous spirit of his bonded him with Sully, it did the opposite with Lizzie, who preferred to stay close to home.

After Cameron and Chloe were born, everything seemed to get worse between them. Bringing children into a shaky marriage never fixes anything, but nobody asked me.

"I've gone over this a thousand times in my head," Lizzie said. "Everything fell apart when Tom just up and left his practice. He didn't even ask me. Did I tell you that, Mother? Not one word. He has a family; there are three other people here to consider."

"He always talked about traveling—"

"New York maybe or England—but Africa? Doctors Without Borders goes to third world countries. It's dangerous; he could be killed and leave the kids without a father. Or what if he got kidnapped? They'd spend the rest of their lives looking for him, wondering what happened. We all would."

"Lizzie, I think you're exaggerating. Tom's a doctor; he'd never do anything foolish or—"

"Are you defending him? Didn't you say he doesn't spend enough time with the kids?"

"Well . . . yes, I did say that. But your father was gone a lot, too."

"Daddy was a policeman, here in town; he worked a regular shift. We knew when he'd be home and when he'd leave. It's not the same. Tom was running out at all hours. I could never count on two days being the same. Even when he went on rounds, there was always some emergency."

"Sorry, honey, but what did you expect when you married a doctor?" Oh, I shouldn't have said that. I took a dill pickle from the plate in front of me and bit off a large bite.

"Are you saying you told me so?"

I shook my head no.

"Because you're not here when he pops in unexpectedly, his arms full of gifts, those Italian eyes of his gleaming. He looks rested, Mother. Can you believe it? Here I am driving the kids to soccer practice, dance lessons, and birthday parties. I'm a chauffeur, a cook, a team leader . . ."

I'd heard the same complaint from so many of my friends throughout the years. We referred to it as the dirty thirties—the age when mothers get all the dirty work. But I commiserated with Lizzie as she vented.

"Cameron almost thinks of his father as a super hero. It isn't fair."

"It certainly is not!" I'd bite my tongue off before I'd give her that worn out adage about life not being fair.

"Thank you." Lizzie said and picked up the remaining half of her sandwich.

"But your life wasn't predictable, either. Running—that's what I remember you always doing. Running to court, running to talk to a client, taking depositions, interviewing witnesses. You certainly can't complain that your life was boring."

She laughed. "Oh no, it was never boring."

"And things are so much better now, right? Switching from criminal to family law was the perfect solution."

"One of the best decisions I've ever made. I just couldn't stand knowing that I was responsible for sending bad guys back out on the street. At first, I thought I was defending the innocent, but later I found out they were few and far between. I was beginning to feel ashamed of myself. I knew I could do more good somewhere else."

It tore at my heart when Lizzie belittled herself like that. "Well your naïveté took one hell of a beating, that's for sure. But just look at you now! Helping battered women, getting those innocent children out of violent situations, you're changing lives. Plus you get to spend more time with the kids—especially Cameron. How's he doing?"

"Good—better than I expected, really. High school has been a big adjustment but he made a friend, Lewis, and they ride the bus together. He goes to speech therapy twice a week. Not that it's been doing much good, as far as I can see, but he needs the routine. Nothing will ever cure the way he stares when he speaks or his emotionless delivery. Kids are always teasing him saying he acts like a robot. But it's all part of his condition."

"He's a smart kid, Lizzie; he'll learn how to work around it. You know, I read every article I can get my hands on. As far as I can see, one doctor has an opinion, the next discredits him, and another has a whole new theory. He'll be just fine."

"I know, but he comes off so . . . distant sometimes. And he's not! He's kind and loving. Plus he's the most creative, almost magical member of this family. He gets that from you and Uncle Nick."

Because of his Asperger's syndrome, my grandson would forever be that proverbial square peg trying to fit into a round hole. But I was confident that eventually he'd be comfortable in his own skin and even use his uniqueness to his advantage. It took me a long time to learn that lesson, but now I was convinced of it.

"And how about our Chloe girl?" I asked.

Lizzie rolled her eyes. "She hates me. According to my darling daughter, I'm unsupportive, the divorce is all my fault, and I only live to humiliate her. Honestly, Mother, she acts like I spend my days plotting against her."

I looked up at the ceiling, acting as though I was trying to dredge up an ancient memory. "Umm. I seem to remember a girl who screamed that her mother was a dictator and had ruined her life. She said that if she couldn't go to a sleepover, her life would be ruined. And then she packed her pink ballerina suitcase and started out the door to go live with her best friend in the world—the only person who really and truly understood her. And let me see . . . what was her friend's name?"

"Candy? Or was it Tammy . . . ?"

"Don't tell me you forgot the name of such an important person!" I said sarcastically. "How can it be that such an earth-shattering event has escaped your memory?"

Lizzie smiled. "Okay, Mother, I get your point."

"Chloe will grow out of this phase but—and remember this part—you have to also. Don't throw all the hurt feelings you've been carrying around at her. She'll get over it and so should you."

"See," she said, "this is why I need you around. To talk me down and keep me sane."

"Oh, honey, you're the sanest person I know."

"I'm not sure if that is always such a good thing."

I could hear the bus screeching to a stop out in front of the house. A moment later, Cameron rushed into the kitchen. When he spotted me sitting there, he abruptly stopped where he was. Those big brown eyes of his lit up.

"Grammy, hi." He kept his distance. Initial meetings always brought out his shyness, even with people he'd known all his life. "I've missed you."

"I missed you, too, Cam. You look like you've grown a foot." I walked to him. "Why, you're almost up to my shoulder. Pretty soon you'll be bigger than any of us." His thick dark hair pointed skyward, held at attention with some sort of gel. Cam came into the world a beautiful baby, and now, when other kids were fighting pimples and braces, he was still my beautiful boy.

"Where's your sister?" Lizzie asked.

"Out front talking to Jennifer, the queen of the neighborhood."

"Why is she the queen?" I asked.

He shrugged his shoulders. "She likes to hold court."

As if on cue, Chloe slowly walked into the room holding an iPhone, her fingers frantically jabbing at the touch screen.

"Chloe, say hello to your grandmother."

Like with all kids her age, it was an effort to tear her eyes away from her phone. "Hey, Grandma."

"Hey, sweetie. You look . . . pretty." I took in the thick strand of purple trailing alongside her shiny red hair. Chloe would never let anyone cut that curly mop of hers. But standing in front of me now was a sullen teenager with short choppy layers all over her head. As I continued to smile, I could see several more piercings running up her ear lobes. And . . . oh no . . . was that a tattoo?

"Thanks, Gram. I like your blouse; it's maj." Then her attention snapped back to her text.

"Chloe, put the phone down and give your grandmother a hug," Lizzie scolded.

She glared at her mother. "Chill, Mom." Then after kissing my cheek, she gave me a polite hug. "Glad you're here, Grandma."

"Me, too, sweetheart."

Cam stood by quietly watching.

"I have presents; I'll go get them."

"I'm supposed to meet up with Jennifer. I'll see you for dinner, okay? We can do the fam thing when I get back."

Lizzie's cheeks reddened. I shot her the look she knew all too well, which warned *Shut up and smile*. "Sure, no prob," I said. Two could play at the short-speak game.

"Dinner's at six." Lizzie shouted at Chloe's back.

I smiled at Cam. "Well, I don't see why you have to wait for your present."

"Me neither."

"Go get the red box on top of my suitcase."

That's all he needed. He was gone like a shot.

"I'm so sorry, Mother. There's no excuse for Chloe's behavior."

"Yes there is. She's thirteen."

Cam walked back into the kitchen, holding the box in front of him like it contained dynamite. "Here it is."

I laid it on the table. Cam pulled a chair close to me and sat. While most kids his age would have been anxious or excited to see what I'd brought, my grandson sat patiently and waited, never saying a word.

I lifted the lid and took out an object wrapped in white tissue paper. Handing it to him, I said, "Careful, it's kind of fragile." Lizzie smiled, enjoying the scene.

He slowly unrolled layer after layer until he finally got to the prize. "What is it?" he asked holding up the miniature figure.

"It's a Kachina doll."

"A doll?"

"Well, they call it that, but it's like your action figures, really. The Hopi Indians believe that everything has a life force. They carve these out of the roots of cottonwood trees. There's lots of different kinds. Animals, ogres, hunters, and warriors. They're said to be spirit messengers of the universe."

"Cool." He picked up the doll and turned it over to examine every detail.

The male figure was mounted on a round wooden base and stood about five inches high. He wore soft buckskin boots that matched a skirt decorated with turquoise and silver beads. His face was covered with a mask made of white feathers, with black ones for the beak. With his outstretched arms also covered in feathers, he resembled a bird in flight.

"The one I picked out for you is the eagle."

"Why the eagle?" Cam asked.

"Because he's the ruler of the sky, the messenger of the heavens. He represents strength and power. And that's how I see you, Cam."

He had to think about that for a minute. Then he said, "Thanks, Grammy." Cam didn't have to force a smile for me to know he was happy with the gift. "Come see my room and we can put Eagle Man in a special place."

"I'm right behind you, sweetheart."

Chapter Three

Resentfully, Chloe came home to eat dinner with us. It was a glorious evening, and I could hear lawn mowers out front of the house. The fresh smell of cut grass was nonexistent in Taos. I'd often missed the bright green of a lush lawn and the passing of seasons since moving to the Southwest. Lizzie plopped steaks on the barbeque while I made a salad in the kitchen. Cam sat at the table with his laptop, reading aloud everything he could find about Kachinas. His enthusiasm delighted me.

After we were all seated out on the deck, Chloe finally put her phone down next to her plate. But she didn't engage in our conversation or even look up to make sure we were still there. Her eyes never left that screen as she chewed her food. I could see Lizzie getting aggravated. Each time I thought
she was going to lose it, I'd start rattling on about something—anything to ease the tension.

"I'm done," Chloe finally announced. "Can I be excused?"

Before Lizzie had a chance to say anything, I spoke. "You never let me give you your present, sweetheart. I'll go get it."

"Okay, Grandma." Before I could even get to my feet, she picked up the phone.

I walked back to the table with a gift wrapped in silver paper. "Here," I said, handing it to her. "Open it."

It was the first time she wasn't texting or looking like she was thinking about texting since I'd arrived. Taking the gift, she quickly ripped the paper off. All the while, she was smiling that dazzling smile of hers. When she'd torn off the last bit of paper, she held up the book. The cover was hand painted, a red and yellow Indian blanket design. As she flipped through the blank pages, the corners of her mouth slowly dropped.

"It's a journal," I said, with an exaggerated enthusiasm. I knew she'd respond in kind for fear of hurting my feelings. And she did.

"Thanks so much, Grandma."

"And there's more!" I told her. Reaching in the pocket of my jean jacket, I pulled out a smaller box. "Here."

Chloe took the gift and this time tore off the wrapping cautiously. "A . . . pen?"

"Not just any pen. It was carved out of a branch from one of the oldest trees in New Mexico. See? The top of yours is a cactus flower. You can write in your journal with it."

Lizzie sat across from me; I could see she was just as confused as her daughter was with my gifts.

"But, Grandma, I have my phone and laptop and—"

"Not anymore, Chloe." I snatched the phone and stuck it deep into my pocket. "While I'm here, you can write all your thoughts—good and bad—in that book. Won't that be fun? Then we can talk about what you wrote. Just you and me."

"You're gonna read what I write? But isn't a journal supposed to be private? And why can't I have my phone? How am I supposed to text my friends?"

"You can do e-mails, or Facebook, whatever you do. Only now you'll have to actually talk to people face to face. And when you're outside the house, I won't have to worry about you walking into traffic or off a cliff." Of course I knew there are no cliffs in Edina, but I was on a roll.

"This is über sick. Mom, tell Grandma how much I need my phone. What if it's an emergency and I have to call you or something. This isn't fair."

"You heard your grandmother." Lizzie looked happy as she sat back in her chair.

"But you're the boss of me, of Cameron, of this whole house—"

"—and Grandma's the boss of me. Sorry."

I got up and hugged Chloe. "You can have the phone back when I leave. But for now, humor an old lady."

"You always do that! Whenever you want to get your way, you say you're old, and we're all supposed to feel bad and do what you say. But you're not old and none of us are falling for it." Then she got up and stomped into the house.

Chloe was my granddaughter all right. She'd caught on to one of my tricks and now I'd have to think up another.

After the kitchen was cleaned up, homework was done, and the kids went to bed, Lizzie and I sneaked out to the deck to enjoy a glass of wine.

"You were brilliant, Mother. Pulling that old good-cop, bad-cop routine on the kids. I had to keep biting my lip so I wouldn't laugh."

"You weren't so bad yourself, counselor. That business about me being the boss of you was a nice touch."

I made the mistake of looking over at her, and once we started laughing, we couldn't stop.

After we'd calmed down, I took a few sips of merlot. "Old tricks are so easy to play on kids 'cause they don't know the punch lines yet. And you need a break, honey. I'll be the bad guy around here for a while to take some of the heat off of you. Consider it your gift."

"You're the best."

"But I do have a bone to pick. Why on earth would you let Chloe get a tattoo? Or all those holes in her precious little ears?"

"Hold on. The tattoo is henna; it washes off after a while. Tom let her get it. And she only has one tiny hole in her ears. That earring just makes it look like a lot. I got it for her for Christmas hoping she'd stop nagging about more piercings."

"Okay, now I can relax."

We sat there for a good ten minutes, just glad to be in the same place at the same time. I thought about how I'd always understand my daughter more completely than she could ever possibly understand me. It was just a fact that I was ahead of her in the timeline of our universe. While I was able to identify with her emotions at every level of her life, she couldn't fathom what I was going through now. And for that reason, I felt a little lonely.

"Oh, did I tell you Dandy Randy is back from New York?" Lizzie asked.

"Randolph Pierce? What's he doing here?"

"He opened an art gallery," Lizzie said, "and he's overseeing renovations at his family's estate. He was always such a cake eater."

"Well, I guess being born into such wealth does sort of warp a person's perspective. Not one single member of the Pierce family is what you'd consider . . . likable. Have you seen him?" I asked.

Lizzie leaned back in her chair. "Yes. The kids and I went out for dinner and Randy was sitting a few tables over." She held her wine glass up, swirling the burgundy liquid slowly around and around. Then she took a sip, knowing very well that when it came to patience, I always came up short.

When I couldn't stand it any longer, I asked, "That's all you're giving me? Come on with the details. What did he look like? What did you talk about?"

She laughed. "He looked good—real good. He was wearing a black leather jacket, black jeans, and a white cashmere sweater. Very minimal. Very New York chic."

"Was he alone?"

"No, he was with an employee—at least that's how he introduced her when he stopped by our table. Her name was Stacey Jordan."

"Pretty?"

"I guess so."

"And is Randolph still a jerk?" I asked.

"No. I was surprised. He said that going to college in New York, getting away from his family, gave him a crack at a fresh start. He loved living where no one knew anything about him."

"So he reinvented himself. Good for him. The Pierce family tree does have some twisted branches," I said. "There were always stories going around about his crazy grandfather and that aunt of his."

"You mean Ms. Jacqueline Bannister-Pierce?" Lizzie pronounced the name in a very proper British accent. "Oh, she moved to Las Vegas after the most recent divorce. Haven't seen her in years."

"Why didn't she move back into the mansion? She could have lived like a queen."

"One of the reasons Randy's back in Edina is because his grandfather's will stipulated that on the centennial of its groundbreaking, the Pierce estate would be transferred to the state of Minnesota."

"Too little, too late."

"Don't go feeling all softhearted for poor Miss Jacqueline, Mother. She has a new man." Lizzie laughed. "And he follows her around like a love-sick puppy."

I have to admit, I was surprised. "Who is he?" I asked.

"Hank Slater. Some muscle bound, washed-up pro football player. Everyone says he sponges off women like Jackie. It's all over the Internet. My paralegal, Kyla, told me she heard that Jackie and Hank came waltzing into Smythe and Albright, looking to hire an attorney."

"She starts at the top, doesn't she? Isn't that the largest law firm in the state?"

"It sure is. She's always felt the family fortune—property and art collections—should have gone to her."

"Well I'm sure old Marshall's will was iron clad."

Lizzie laughed. "Bulletproof from what I've heard."

Chapter Four

"Mom," Chloe whined, "Cam's eating all the cereal."

"Am not," I could hear my grandson say in a calm, even tone.

"Are too!"

"Quiet. You're going to wake Grammy up," he told her.

"Shhh, both of you," Lizzie whispered.

"OMG, Mom. Can't you make Grandma give my phone back? Pleeease? Daddy gave that to me 'cause I got all Bs. He'd be crazy mad if he knew."

Her mother didn't take the bait, only asking her if she was finished eating.

Way to go, Lizzie, I thought and wondered if the three of them were aware that I could hear every word they were saying. Probably not. Their rooms were separated from the kitchen by a long hallway. But mine was just on the other side of the wall. I bet they didn't have a clue.

For a minute, I thought of getting up, putting on my robe, and rushing out to wish them all a good day. But that thought went away as I stretched my feet across the luxurious sheets.

Their conversation stopped suddenly but was immediately followed by the clanking of silverware hitting the stainless steel sink. The refrigerator seemed to open and close nonstop. Chairs skidded across the tiled floor until finally, thank goodness, Lizzie said, "Now grab your lunches and get in the car. I have to go to the office, so I can drive you to school, but you'll have to take the bus home."

"Shotgun!" Chloe shouted.

Cameron was silent.

I could hear one child run toward the front of the house; the other slowly followed. When the door slammed shut, I thought they were gone, until I heard a knock.

"Mother, I know you heard everything."

"Yes, I did."

Through the door, Lizzie said, "You have my cell number and the one at the office. I should be home late. Could you please feed the kids dinner?"

"No problem."

"Thanks so much. Love you."

"Love you, too, sweetheart," I called back.

Curiosity finally made me get out of bed. Hearing that Randolph Pierce had opened an art gallery piqued my interest, and I decided to check it out. But first I had a cup of coffee and piece of toast while I looked for the spare keys to Sully's jeep.

The Grand Cherokee was only a few months old

with less than five thousand miles on it when he died. Neither Lizzie nor I could bear to look at it back then. But we couldn't part with it, either. So it sat on his side of the garage until I sold our house, and then it got moved to Lizzie's garage. When our grief finally turned into acceptance, we both felt comforted knowing it was there.

After a nice hot shower, I pulled a sweater over my head, stepped into my favorite jeans, and then hiked up a pair of soft leather boots. The turquoise necklace I added looked silly here in Minnesota, so I took it off. My hair was getting too long; I'd need a haircut soon. After applying a little makeup, I was ready.

My one luxury—well a necessity, really, considering all the traveling I did—was a smartphone. (The irony of taking Chloe's phone away from her did not escape me.) But in order to find the location of the gallery, I had to know its name. Randolph Pierce had told Lizzie he'd "found himself" while living in New York. I never understood that term. It's exhausting how much energy people spend losing and finding themselves. Anyway, if what he said about hating his family was true, the gallery would have an artsy, pretentious name—anything but Pierce. On the other hand, since Randolph always had such an inflated ego, I ultimately searched for Pierce Gallery.

Bingo.

• • •

The intersection of Fiftieth and France, in historic Edina, features some of the best shopping in the Twin Cities area. You can find anything from lingerie to fine wine. Pierce Art Gallery was sandwiched between a French bistro and an upscale jewelry store. The façade of the building was yellow brick. Over the ornate front door hung a wide, black awning, announcing the gallery's name in fancy gray letters.

As I stepped inside, a buzzer went off in a back room. Before I could take a dozen steps, a petite woman walked casually toward me. She was wearing a short leather skirt, a tight black blouse, and stilettos so high I wondered how she managed to move so gracefully. Her hair was cut short—too short. From a distance, I guessed her age to be between eighteen and twenty. But as she got closer, I could see she was no teenager and probably closer to thirty.

"May I help you?" she asked, smiling an over-friendly grin.

"Is Randolph here?"

"Well . . . he's very busy. Can I tell him what it's about?"

"He went to school with my daughter; I've known him since he was a kid. When I heard he'd opened an art gallery, well, I had to come see it."

"Oh, a family friend?"

That would be stretching the truth considerably, but I just nodded.

"I'll let him know you're here. Mrs. . . ."

"Katherine Sullivan, hi." I held out my hand and was impressed when she offered a firm shake, rattling the large, colorful bracelet on her wrist.

"And I'm Stacey Jordan. Are you by any chance Lizzie's mother? The chief of police?"

"In the flesh. And I'm retired now."

"I met your daughter and her kids at dinner the other night. What a beautiful family. You must be so proud of Lizzie, her being a lawyer, working with autistic children in that art therapy program. I'm hoping to get involved with the project somehow."

"Lizzie told me that you recently graduated with a degree in art conservation. Now that's impressive."

She shrugged off my compliment, looking uncomfortable with the praise. "I've always loved anything having to do with art. And I'm lucky that I get to work part time here and with Mr. Rousseau over at the mansion."

"Rousseau? I'm not familiar with that name."

"Antoine Rousseau. He lives in France but travels all around the world overseeing special projects. He's the best art conservator alive today." She took a step closer. "But just between you and me, Antoine can be a real handful.

He's an obsessive-compulsive—very meticulous. Maybe geniuses are all just . . ."

"Quirky," I finished. "It's the best way to describe someone who's a bit off center. When I was a rookie, we'd say 'kook' or 'nut-job.' But now everything has to be politically correct."

Stacey laughed. "Well, then, Mr. Rousseau is the most 'quirky' person I've ever met."

I liked Stacey. She was obviously beautiful but, more important, energetic and smart. "Aren't you tempted to snoop around that place?" I asked her. "You know, peek behind the Wizard's curtain? I know I would be. There are so many stories about Pierce mansion."

She rolled her eyes. "I could probably write a book about all I've seen out there. You wouldn't believe—"

"Stacey!" Randolph Pierce snapped as he walked out from what I assumed was his office in the back of the gallery.

He had that casual look people work so hard to perfect. His sandy brown hair was cut close to his head. Beneath an expensive black sport coat, he wore a T-shirt tucked into a pair of tight-fitting jeans. He finished off his look with tasseled loafers and, of course, no socks. But his face was the surprise. Maybe there were a few wrinkles around his eyes and he'd put on a few pounds, but the forty-year-old man that stood in front of me looked exactly as he had when he was sixteen. I would have recognized Randolph Pierce any-where, any day.

"Don't you have some work to do?" His outburst made the other customers in the gallery look over at our threesome.

Stacey held back her embarrassment remarkably well. "It was so nice meeting you, Mrs. Sullivan."

"You too, Stacey. Maybe we can have coffee . . . or a drink sometime?"

"I'd like that." She gave me a weak smile.

Randolph glared at the girl as she walked away. I couldn't help wondering what was going on between the two of them. As soon as Stacey was out of sight, he turned to me, all smiles.

"Mrs. Sullivan? It's been a long time. You look great. Lizzie told me you were coming into town for a while." Then he grabbed me into a quick hug. "It's so good to see you."

"You too, Randolph. You haven't changed a bit . . . I mean it."

"Well, I don't know about that, but it's so nice of you to stop in."

"When Lizzie told me you'd opened a gallery, I had to come see it."

"That's right; you're an artist now."

"I've always been an artist," I told him. "I studied and took all kinds of courses. When we needed some extra cash, I even thought of being a forensic sketch artist. Life just took me into another direction. But now that I'm retired and

Sully's gone, the old artist in me has been resurrected."

"I was so sorry to hear about Mr. Sullivan. What a shock. Please accept my condolences."

"Thank you, Randolph. That's very kind of you."

"Mr. Sullivan was always fair with me; I admired him greatly."

"If I remember correctly, the last time he brought you in was when the Jergens family called, claiming you vandalized their lake house."

Randolph was not the typical bad boy back then. He'd been raised by nannies; his parents were always out of the country or too busy to spend time with him. And there was a certain sense of entitlement that came along with the Pierce name. No matter what the poor kid did, it seemed he was despised by everyone in Edina. I suppose that after a while, it was easier for him to just stop trying and do whatever he wanted.

"I was so angry back then. Always trying to prove I wasn't like my family. I did some stupid things."

I saw he was getting upset, so I didn't push it. "Well, that was then," I said. "Look at you now."

He beamed. "So you approve?"

"Oh, the place is beautiful but . . . I was surprised when I first walked in."

"Surprised? Why?" he asked, confused.

"Knowing how your family collected classical

art, I just thought that's what you'd have here. But now I see you're into more modern and abstract works."

He glanced at the wall behind me. "And you don't like it?"

"No, I didn't mean that. I love the Kandinsky over there and that Stella—he's my favorite pop artist. The abstracts are fantastic . . . Salvador Dalí is spectacular. It's just not what I paint and definitely not what I'd expect you to like."

"Oh, I hated visiting my grandfather at that musty old mansion. Everything was so valuable—don't touch, don't run, don't sit on that chair because it belonged to some king or was made by a famous craftsman. The only thing missing were those velvet ropes they have in a museum to keep people out."

"So how did you come to open your own gallery?"

"After switching my major from economics—my dad's idea—to art history, it opened up a whole new world. I got into the gallery scene in lower Manhattan, met creative, liberal people. It was exhilarating. I'd go to lectures and gallery openings. It was incredible. So I purchased a gallery in the Meatpacking District, which led to me funding an art and technology collective."

"You've been a busy boy, Randolph. And along the way, you must have made some great friends."

His expression changed. "I guess so."

I wondered what he was hiding, but before I could ask another question, the phone in his breast pocket rang.

It was an automatic reflex that made him pull the phone out and look down at the number calling. "I'm sorry. I have to take this," he told me. "Look around. There's some cucumber water in that carafe over there. I'll be right back." He smiled graciously and walked to the back of the gallery.

Being alone gave me a few minutes to look around the room. The front of the shop was all glass and the three brick walls were painted matte black. Moldings and baseboards were burnished silver. A huge chandelier made of silver discs of all sizes hung in the middle of the ceiling, which was also black. The floor was covered in a dusky grey carpet. Two leather director's chairs were positioned next to a glass table in a corner. Sleek, modern, sterile, and cold is what the decorator was obviously going for— which was smart. It showcased the colorful, surreal paintings that hung at all levels on the walls.

I drew my attention to a small Picasso lithograph, something from his blue period, surrounded by a grouping of up-and-coming contemporary artists. It was near the corner where Randolph stood talking on his phone. I didn't want to appear to be eavesdropping, but it was difficult not to overhear when his voice rose.

"No! I told you I can't do that! Why would you even ask? I'm not going to tell . . ." He trailed off when I caught his eye.

I motioned that I had to leave.

He covered the mouthpiece. "I'd love to see your work sometime."

"Sure," I called to him, then waved good-bye and hurried out of the gallery. Something just didn't feel right in there and I knew better than to ignore my instincts.

Chapter Five

I'd started my day planning to indulge in a leisurely lunch, but after rushing out of the Pierce Gallery, I felt too keyed up to relax. Now all I wanted was to just get some food in my stomach. When I spotted a place on the corner, I steered the Cherokee toward the drive-in window. After paying for my order, I parked in a spot that would afford me some good people-watching time.

Halfway through my cheeseburger, I realized I hadn't recognized any of the faces passing by. And as I finished the last fry, it dawned on me that once upon a time, a pet store had been on this corner.

If you want to really see how much a place has changed, leave it for a while. If you've lived on the same street in the same town for most of your life, change happens very slowly. A house you drive by every day is just part of the landscape. Over time, it slowly deteriorates, its occupants move out, the fence falls down. Each day, it's taking up less space. One day a construction crew shows up out front, and maybe one of their trucks catches your attention. But within a few days, their presence is expected and taken for granted. All this happens over the course of a month or year. Finally, there's only a vacant lot, spotted with two industrial-size dumpsters and some workers cleaning up the mess. That takes a few more weeks. And now when you drive by, you've been conditioned to not expect to see the house anymore. Soon you can't remember that it was even there.

Now imagine you've been away for a few years. You drive by the old neighborhood expecting to see the Johnson house that's forever fixed in your childhood memories. But now it's gone. Just vanished overnight. And you're stunned.

It was a chilly afternoon, but the sun was bright and warmed my face as I drove down streets I'd traveled most of my life. Checking the clock in the dashboard, I realized there was still plenty of time to get my hair cut before the kids got home from school.

I'd gone to The Beauty Mark and taken Lizzie there for years. It was owned and operated by a high school friend of mine, Margaret Ann Wilson. After graduation, we had gone to Minneapolis to finish our educations—she to cosmetology school and I to the police academy. As soon as Margaret Ann completed her training, she rented a store-front, hired a decorator, and set up shop.

The Beauty Mark was elegant yet comfortable. There were three kinds of coffee available to customers, fresh pastries, and the latest issues of all the best magazines. The girls who worked there were constantly going to beauty shows to learn the latest styles and cuts. As I got closer to the salon, I was eager to see my friend and hear the latest gossip.

But when I turned down the familiar street, I could see the façade of the small building had been transformed into a Fabulous Cuts. The large flowerpots, normally brimming over with seasonal plants, were gone. And I was not only surprised but a little hurt that Margaret Ann hadn't told me about this big change in her life. We used to share everything.

I hesitated for a minute. My hair only needed a slight trim; it wouldn't take that long. And I was right in front of the place. So I parked in front of the bushel of balloons that decorated the store-front and locked the car.

As I pushed the door open, I just hoped something would look familiar. The walls had been covered with celebrity head shots; the black and white movie stills that used to hang there were gone. The spot where the coffee station had been was now taken up with shelves of products: shampoos, conditioners, thickeners, and sprays.

"Katherine Sullivan! Is that you?"

There she sat, behind the receptionist's desk.

"Margaret Ann Wilson!" As I walked over to

her, she ran out from behind the desk and hugged me.

"I haven't seen you since your retirement party. Last I heard from Lizzie, you were living in the Southwest."

"For now," I said. "And the last time I saw you this place was still The Mark. What happened?"

"One sweet deal is what happened. The location is perfect and our clients are loyal. After a few meetings, we came up with a price with the stipulation that I still manage the shop. It's all good."

Her joy was contagious, and I smiled with her. "I'm so glad it all worked out for you."

"So is this a social or professional visit?" she asked.

"Professional."

"Well set your fanny down and let's see what we can do."

While my hair got washed, dried, and trimmed, Margaret Ann chattered away, filling me in on all the local news. Throughout our conversation, one name kept coming up: Dean Bostwick, the man who'd replaced me as chief of police.

"That son-of-a-you-know-what, always telling anyone who'd listen that you were too old for the job. We all hated him, Kate. You know we were always on your side, right?"

"Oh, there weren't any sides to be on. He was a good cop and deserved the promotion."

"And you're still so nice, even after all the hell

he put you through. I'm surprised Sully never took a swing at him."

I laughed. "He wanted to but I've always been able to fight my own battles."

"You certainly have."

"Have you checked out the Pierce Art Gallery? I just came from there."

Margaret Ann stopped trimming my hair. Standing back, she said, "Not my scene, but since you mentioned the Pierce family, do you know who's in town?"

"Other than Randolph?"

"Jacqueline—she's such a pathetic, crazy lady. Reminds me of Gloria Swanson in that old movie *Sunset Boulevard*. She gives me the creeps walking around town in that mangy coat of hers, all made up like she's going out on the town instead of just to the drug store."

"Remember when she was married to that producer; they lived in Hollywood next to Jimmy Stewart? Her picture was always in the society pages, showing her at some premiere or Washington fundraiser. She was so delicate, so glamorous . . . and rich."

Margaret nodded. "I remember reading something about an actor drowning in her swimming pool when she was living in Rome."

"That would have been her fourth husband."

"But she always had Randy, her favorite nephew," she said.

"The two last surviving members of the Pierce family."

Jacqueline's father had died years before. He always blamed her for the death of her younger brother, Leland. Marshall Senior was horrible to everyone, but Jackie got the worst of it.

After another ten minutes, she put her scissors down. "There, how's that?"

I looked myself over. "Perfect."

"Do you color your hair? There's not a speck of grey that I could see. You must do something."

"For Redheads Only, number two-oh-five, crimson sunset." I shrugged, "It keeps me young and costs a lot less than a facelift would."

"Don't you ever go under the knife!" she commanded. "You've always been a knockout, Kate, and always will be. You're just one of those natural beauties that make the rest of us look bad."

"Is this the part where I'm supposed to feel sorry for the successful business woman? The same person who was head cheerleader? The homecoming queen? Miss Teen Minnesota? Get real."

After we got done stroking each other's egos, I took out my wallet.

"Oh no, you don't. It's on the house."

"And I'll take it." I laughed. "Thanks."

We promised to be better with phone calls and texts. She told me she'd try to come out and visit me before winter. But we both knew she never traveled outside her home state.

I was putting a chicken and rice casserole in the oven when I heard the kids come in the front door.

"How was school?" I asked.

Chloe stuck out that bottom lip of hers. "It sucked. Jennifer thinks she's all that, just because she's got a stupid boyfriend. All she ever talks about is that lame-oh nerd."

Cameron shrugged.

I walked over to Chloe and smoothed her hair. "Well, you're going to have plenty of boyfriends, luv, you'll see."

"But I don't have one now. And even if I did, I couldn't talk to him on account of I don't even have a phone." She shot me a dirty look but didn't move away from my touch.

No matter how angry she got, I had to stay strong. So I acted as though her bad mood was having no effect on me. "I made chicken and rice for dinner."

Cameron hugged me. "Thanks, Grammy."

"You're welcome, sweetheart. Do you have homework?"

"I did it in study hall," he said.

"How long 'til we eat?" Chloe asked, separating herself from me and her brother.

"About an hour."

"I'll watch TV now and do homework later."

As she bolted out of the room, I called after her. "I'll let you know when it's ready."

"Whatevs," she said under her breath.

"Sisters are very complicated," Cameron said.

"I hear that," I said. Then, noticing the sketch pad sticking out of his backpack, I asked, "Can I see what you're working on?"

He took out the pad and laid it on the table. "Let me get rid of this," he said holding up his backpack. Then he went to his bedroom.

My grandson and I had spent many hours together drawing. I'd learned early on that it was the best way to get him to open up to me. It was his comfort zone, and I hoped that he would always have it and that it would always be something that we could share.

When he pulled out a chair, I sat down on the one next to it. After he got comfortable, he flipped the notebook open.

"Wow, so you're into pencil now. Last time I was here, it was colored markers. Big bold pictures with lots of super heroes."

He nodded. "That was years ago, when I was a baby."

It was only last winter, but who was I to argue?

I held the picture closer, admiring the extraordinary details he'd obviously worked on for hours. "It looks just like this kitchen. Every tile in the floor, so exact. You have a remarkable sense of proportion, Cam. I can read the labels on every spice jar in the rack on the wall. It's almost like a photograph. You have all the cabinets and knobs, every magnet on the refrigerator. Do you realize how talented you are?"

He looked up at me, and when our eyes met, he smiled. It was a glorious moment to feel so connected to him.

"But what's up with the ceiling?" I asked, scrutinizing the sketch again. "Why does it have birds and branches on it?"

"It's a convertible ceiling, like in Dad's car. You can open it up and see the sky and trees that hang over the roof."

"What made you think of that?"

"I wanted it to be easier for Dad to come see us. He's always so busy, on a plane going some-where else. I just thought if he looked down and saw all of us inside, waiting for him, that he'd want to come here more. And maybe if he saw how much we miss him, he'd never want to leave."

My heart was breaking as I realized how much the divorce was affecting him. "I think that's a great idea. Maybe every house should have a convertible ceiling." I tried lightening his mood but it wasn't working.

"It would also make it easier for him to fly away when he's done with us."

I leaned over and hugged him. "Your father

will never be done with you. You know that, don't you?"

"I guess. But it still makes me feel bad."

"Do you and Chloe ever go visit him?" I asked.

"Sometimes. But his apartment's real small and we don't have our stuff there."

"Maybe, when you're older, you can go on a trip with him. That would be exciting, wouldn't it? You'd always have your mom here at home, making sure your things are safe in your room. And she'd always be here to welcome you back. But you'd also have a dad who takes you on adventures. Maybe a safari in Africa, or a boat ride down the Nile. That way you'd have the best of both worlds."

Cam shook his head. "He doesn't like me sometimes. I can tell. He wouldn't want to take me on any kind of trip."

"Oh, that isn't true." I wanted to cry but kept a stupid smile plastered across my face. "Why would you think such a thing? Has he ever told you that?"

"He doesn't have to. I can feel it."

Cam had always been the quietest kid in any room and the most sensitive one.

All I could do was hug him tighter.

"You know your father loves you and Chloe to pieces. He's just not like you and me. He's a very practical, serious man. He has to know procedures and medicines . . . lots to remember.

It's all very important work. If he messes up, his patient might die. Not like us artists. If we mess up, we can just paint over our mistakes or erase them."

He sat up and smiled. "I know. But, Grammy, why does everything have to change?"

"You know, Cam, I was wondering about change myself today. It's never easy, is it?"

Chapter Six

Both kids were quiet during dinner. Cameron was quiet because that was his nature and Chloe because she was thirteen and still angry with me. I tried several times to start a conversation but got nowhere. After the dishes were cleared away and I brought out the chocolate cake, I finally got a reaction. Chocolate is a happy food—it's a scientific fact.

In spite of herself, Chloe smiled as she licked icing off her fingers and Cameron told us about a baking show he liked to watch on the Food Network. But when the treat was gone, so were their sunny moods.

Cameron took his dish to the sink. "I'm going to my room now, okay Grammy?"

"Sure, honey. Your mom said you go to bed at nine. I'll be in to say good night."

"Okay." He left the room.

"Dinner was good, Grandma, thanks." When Chloe started toward her bedroom, I stopped her.

"Come sit with me. We haven't had a chance to visit—just the two of us." As I expected, she heaved a heavy sigh and slowly, grudgingly walked back to the kitchen.

I smiled, acting as though I hadn't noticed her demeanor, and patted the chair next to me.

She threw herself down on the seat. "Will this take long? I have homework."

"Do you know what I was thinking on the flight here?"

"No," she said, staring down at her shoes, kicking her feet back and forth.

"I was wondering, what can I do to make Chloe miserable? What can I say to make her really mad at me? And I tried to think of something horrible but—"

"I don't hate you," she said in a sarcastic tone.

"Darn. I must be losing it." I made a serious face and pretended to be upset with myself. "Guess I'll have to try harder. 'Cause my only reason for visiting you and your brother and mother is to make all of you thoroughly miserable. And when the three of you are unhappy, I'm good."

She finally looked up, and the confusion in her eyes was delicious to see. Now maybe we could have a real conversation.

"Why would you want to make us all miserable?" she asked.

"Have I ever done anything intentionally to be mean to you? Ever?"

The arrogance was gone now and she answered in a tiny voice. "No . . . never."

"So why would I start now?"

"But you took my phone. Daddy gave me that phone—it's mine."

"Is that the only thing he's ever given you?" I asked. "You mean to tell me he's never given you presents for your birthday or Christmas? What about Easter and Valentine's Day? Nothing?"

"That was before—when he lived with us. The phone was the first thing he gave me when he moved away. It's special 'cause he bought it just for me, so we can talk or text—whenever."

"So if I looked up the call history on that phone, the only number I'd find would be your dad's, right?"

"Well . . . and maybe some friends. But you can check, Grandma. I call Dad every day, swear."

"I'm not going to check up on you, Chloe. I trust you." I held my arms open. She didn't come to me, as I'd hoped, but she started to cry.

"I know you'd never hurt me. But I used to think Mom and Daddy wouldn't either. Now he's far away taking care of all the sick people in the world, leaving me alone here. I'm just so mad at him!"

"You're not alone, sweetie. You have your mom and your big brother."

Chloe straightened up, swiping at her tears with the sleeve of her sweatshirt. "Mom's never here anymore. Not since she got all involved with her *important* work. All she cares about is helping other kids and their mothers. And if she isn't worried about some strangers, she's worried about Cam. I know he's got Asperger's, everyone knows, that's all she talks about. But he gets good grades—better than mine. It's not like he's gonna die or anything."

"You feel left out," I said.

She nodded. "Majorly."

"Have you told Mom any of this?"

"I try. But sometimes I think she'd like me better if I was sick. Then maybe I'd be important like those other kids."

"Come on, you know that isn't true. Don't you?"

"Maybe."

I leaned back and studied my sweet Chloe girl. "You know, you're strong and fearless like all the women in this family are. You can accomplish anything. I never give up, your mom's always been a fighter, and you're just like her. But along with the good comes the bad. It isn't easy being us."

"What's the bad part?" she asked.

"People just assume we don't need help because we don't ask for it. So they move on to someone they think needs them more than we do. But they're wrong. People like us do need help, just in smaller doses. And we get afraid like everyone else but try not to show it."

"Mom's not afraid of anything," Chloe grumbled.

"See? Because she tries to stay strong for you and your brother, you assume she doesn't need your kindness. But she does."

"What about me?" she asked. "Maybe we'd all be better off if I just went to live with Daddy."

"Didn't you just tell me he's hardly ever home?"

She thought about that a moment.

"And his apartment's small. All your stuff's here, right?" I asked.

"Yes."

"Look, Chloe, it doesn't matter where you live; you're always going to be a member of this family. You're always going to have a brother and a mother and father. A different address won't change a thing."

"But . . . I think it would be cool."

"Maybe you're right. A girl like you wouldn't have trouble fitting in at a new school, I guess. You've always been good at making friends. And when your dad's out of town, you're old enough to cook for yourself, clean the apartment, and do the laundry . . ."

That did it. Her eyes grew bigger with each challenge I threw at her.

"I'm only thirteen; I can't live by myself."

"But you're so miserable here," I said.

"It's not that bad."

"Why don't you have a nice long talk with your mother? I bet she doesn't even know how her work makes you feel."

"Could you?"

"No prob. Now why don't you go do your homework?"

Chloe stood up and walked over to me. "You're cool, Grandma."

"I try."

I was watching the news when Lizzie got home a little after ten. I'd left a place set for her at the kitchen table and went to heat up the leftovers from dinner after she hung up her coat.

"So how was your day?" I asked, pouring myself a glass of wine.

"Exhausting. I don't know how you did it for all those years, Mother. A woman came in this afternoon with her three children—all under the age of five. Her husband locked her in everyday before he went to work, and today she'd had enough, so she grabbed the kids and ran. She has no money, no place to live."

I took her plate out of the microwave. "So what happened?"

"We coordinate with several shelters but it's hard finding a place that will take the kids, too. My assistant Josh and I worked for hours, making calls. All the time she's hysterical that the bastard will find her. I kept assuring her she was safe. And just when we're getting in the car to move her, she decides to go back home."

"She wasn't ready," I said.

"It's so frustrating. I'll never understand—"

"—It's not your job to understand her; you're not a therapist, Lizzie. All you can do is be there when she's ready." I walked to the table with her food and my wine.

"I know. But that doesn't make it any easier."

"It certainly does not."

Lizzie started to eat while I sat down. "So what's been going on here?" she asked.

I told her about my conversations with Chloe and Cameron. At first, she just listened and nodded. But after she heard that Chloe was thinking about moving in with Tom, she got defensive. By the time I was finished, she admitted that she should slow down a bit and spend more time with both of them.

"Do you have room for dessert?" I asked when her plate was clean.

"Please say there's chocolate cake with double chocolate icing."

"Do I know my daughter or what?" I got up to cut her a slice.

"You're an angel." Lizzie sat back and relaxed her shoulders. "So, tell me what you did before the kids got home, besides getting your hair cut. It looks great, by the way. I'm guessing you went to The Mark."

"How come you never mentioned, not one single time, during any of our many conversations, that the place is now a Fabulous Cuts?"

"Oh, it's basically the same. Margaret Ann still runs the show."

"And she still looks great. Once a beauty queen, always a beauty queen, I guess."

We laughed.

"Talking about looking the same, I went to the Pierce Gallery this morning. Randolph was there. He's still as handsome as ever."

"What did you think of the place?" she asked.

"I was expecting something more traditional, but I liked it. And you were right; he does seem more down to earth. His assistant is cute."

"So you met the beautiful and oh-so-talented Stacey? I thought she spent most of her valuable time at the mansion."

Was I detecting a hint of jealousy? "Not today, I guess."

"What did you and Randy talk about?"

"New York, the gallery . . . stuff like that. But then he got a phone call and needed privacy, so he scurried off to a corner. Which was weird considering he has an office and it was obviously a personal call."

"What made you think it was personal?"

"Well one minute he's charming, going on and on about his new outlook on life. Happy and relaxed. Then he gets that call and turns into a maniac. He's shouting, waving his arms, telling someone to stop nagging him."

"Randy's always been . . . eccentric," Lizzie said, concentrating on the last few bites of her cake.

"But why didn't he just go in the back? He obviously knew who the caller was; I saw him check the screen before he answered the phone. There were other customers in the gallery, and he didn't seem to care if he was making a scene. Why would he—"

"Mother," Lizzie put down her fork. "What do you care? You're retired now; stop analyzing every situation."

Her remark irritated me, but before I could say anything in response, the doorbell rang. "I'll get it," I said, hoping to walk off my anger.

I looked through the peephole. Standing on the other side of the door was Nathan Walker, Sully's former partner and one of my closest friends.

"Nathan!" I said as I opened the door. "What a surprise."

"Kathy!" He rushed forward and gave me a big hug.

"What are you doing here so late?"

"I was hoping you were up. There's been a murder at the Pierce estate."

Chapter Seven

I considered Nathan Walker my best friend and confidant. He was with Sully that day at the bank when two gunmen took nine hostages. It had been snowing off and on for days, schools were closed, and public transportation had ceased altogether. I've often thought those idiots intentionally staged the robbery on that day, thinking the bad weather would slow down the cops. But bad men are usually stupid men, and they never considered how the snow would hamper their escape. Sully and Nathan were just finishing up their shift when they were called to the scene. Although I also responded, they were first on the scene and in charge.

The robbers released seven hostages. Each time, either Sully or Nathan would rush the frightened victim into a squad car where it was warm. It went on like that until we all thought the perps were close to surrendering.

Sully was up front when Sidney Lang, the bank manager, was released. The frightened man stumbled toward Sully and then slid on a patch of ice, falling backward, hitting his head. That's when all hell broke loose.

Gunshots echoed off the granite buildings; I thought I'd go deaf. Even though we'd roped off the area, rubbernecks gathered. I tried to stay calm and in control, but for a few horrible moments, it was utter chaos.

Then deafening quiet.

Sully was down and I ran to him, shouting to the EMTs to hurry. Then I gave the order to rush the building.

There were two casualties that day: one of the robbers . . . and my husband.

Eventually Nathan's survivor's guilt rendered him useless out on the street and I put him behind a desk. The police psychiatrist ordered us both to take a month's leave and attend weekly sessions. But we'd been around too long and had heard the same tired phrases the shrink threw at us too many times for any of it to stick. Our strength was in each other, the shared bond we had loving Sully.

We'd go to the sessions because they were mandatory, but the real healing came when we talked one on one. We could cry together without any embarrassment, say anything without fear of being judged or having our words repeated.

When Nathan heard about a police veteran who was looking to sell his security business and move to Florida, he didn't think twice about retiring and buying it.

Somehow I managed to handle my duties as chief for a few more years until realizing I could easily retire and never look back. I had Lizzie and the kids to occupy some of my time. I broke out the art supplies and took a few watercolor classes. Sometimes I'd invite Nathan and his beautiful wife, Terry, over for dinner. Sometimes I'd go to their place. But without Sully, it all seemed so frivolous, just filler to take up time.

Then one day another of those travel brochures arrived. But that one wasn't for a cruise to Mexico or a helicopter tour of the Hawaiian Islands. There was an artist's retreat in Maine. The pictures showed six cabins scattered throughout a ten-acre area. A large meeting hall was available for three meals a day as well as group discussions. I was on a plane the following week.

Nathan and I communicated daily either by phone or e-mail, just to make sure the other was doing well. Our conversations gradually became less full of Sully and more full of the adventures we were both having in our new lives. I'd been at the retreat ten days when he called to tell me Terry had died.

Of course, I offered to fly home immediately, but he told me to stay put. If I came back to Edina, he said, it would be like replaying Sully's death. He needed to grieve with his family; he had to make it different this time. And so I respected his wishes. But I still called everyday just to talk him through his loss.

After that, whenever I was in town, we'd meet. He'd ask about what I was working on and listen attentively as I described a new piece or gush over a new artist I'd recently discovered. I'd listen while he talked about the security business and the two men and two women he liked to call his crew.

"We're both retired, you know," I told Nathan as he drove toward the mansion.

"Just because we're out to pasture doesn't mean we can't jump the fence every now and then." He laughed.

"I know that. And you know that. But your timing couldn't be worse. I was just getting a lecture from my daughter. She was complaining that I'm always profiling and analyzing."

"And are you?" he asked.

"Of course. But that's not a bad thing . . . is it?"

"Look who you're asking." When he smiled, he always reminded me of Denzel Washington. It didn't matter that he was now sixty-four or had a few scars across his cheek and some extra pounds around the middle. He was still a ruggedly handsome man. The women at the station had been crazy for him. But back then, Nathan only had eyes for his wife.

"So how did you find out about the murder?" I asked.

"We have a police scanner at the office. A call came in about half an hour ago that a body was found on the second floor of the Pierce estate. The police are there now."

"Do you have any idea who it is?" I asked.

"I would if Randolph would have let me install a surveillance system in the place."

"You mean there isn't one?" I asked, surprised. "That's insane, considering all the artwork and antiques they have."

"Oh, there's a system all right, but it's ancient. Old man Marshall was the last Pierce to live full-time in the mansion. Just him, a nurse, a housekeeper, and some old coot—"

"—Bradley. He was Marshall's butler for years—very protective."

Nathan nodded. "Sure, I remember him. Anyway, after the old man died—"

"—under mysterious circumstances," I interjected.

"There was never proof of any wrongdoing, but it was strange," he agreed.

"And the bulk of his estate went to Junior," I said. "With one stipulation."

Nathan glanced over at me. "I never heard anything about that."

"Lizzie told me. A lawyer friend of hers drew up the original will. And since attorney–client privilege doesn't cover this . . ."

"So . . . tell me."

"It stipulated that on the centennial of the groundbreaking of the estate, which is this year, it would be transferred back to the town of Edina. Did you know it was originally named Buckhorn manor?"

"After all those poisonous plants around here?" Nathan asked.

I nodded. "They used to make paint out of them."

"Seems fitting somehow. Marshall Senior seemed to poison everything he touched, all the time adding more to his daddy's wealth. It's never enough with those kinds of people. Everyone in town has a relative who was affected by his ruthlessness."

"Did you ever have a conversation with the man?" I asked Nathan. "To hear him talk, he was a benevolent industrialist who was only trying to push the United States into the modern age. Never mind that he profited from the Depression and the war. There was even a rumor that he purchased stolen art from the Nazis. Nothing was beneath him."

"Yeah, the old man was a real piece of work," Nathan said. "And no one's lived in the manse ever since. From what I've heard, anything of value was cleared out and stored long ago."

"And now Randolph's in town, renovating Buckhorn, getting it ready to be turned into a museum, I suppose."

Nathan parked in front of the huge building. "Once everything's back in place, he'll realize he needs top-of-the-line security. Especially after what happened here tonight."

We sat in the car for a few minutes and checked out the scene. Three squad cars were parked at odd angles across the gravel driveway that fanned out in front of the building, two with their lights flashing. An ambulance had been backed up as far as it could go to the front door. I could see an EMT leaning against the side of the ambulance smoking a cigarette. Yellow police tape had been wrapped around one of the tall white columns flanking the hand-carved door. Then it had been stretched and wrapped tightly around the opposite column. Two more strips of tape formed a large X across the entrance. Without another word between us, we got out of the car and walked up the long driveway.

Chapter Eight

My old take-charge attitude kicked in. "You occupy him while I go inside," I told Nathan, pointing to the EMT.

"Whatever you say, Chief," he joked. "If you need me, just holler."

The EMT looked at me with mild interest and nodded. Hopefully giving the impression that I belonged there, I ducked under the police tape.

"Nathan Walker—Walker Security. Can I ask you a few questions?" I heard Nathan say to the man as I opened the front door.

I was inside before the EMT had a chance to answer.

Dusty, paint-spattered tarps covered the floor in the foyer. A small chandelier draped with a sheet had been turned on and gave the room an eerie appearance. It felt as though I was standing inside a large skeleton as I looked at the scaffolds surrounding me. Walls were spotted with gray plaster; in some spots, drywall was exposed. What a difference from the last time I'd visited the mansion when Marshall Senior was alive. I could hear voices on the second floor and started toward the staircase, also covered with cream-colored tarps.

The second floor, unlike the first, was so lit

up I had to stop a moment to let my eyes adjust.

"Well look who's here!" a voice called. "Chief Sullivan! Long time, no see."

I'd recognize that raspy voice anywhere. "Officer DeYoung," I said, walking toward him. "You still partnered with Browman?"

"Some things never change, Chief. I thought you moved away from our little burg."

"You can take the girl out of Edina but . . . you get it," I laughed. "So what have we got here?"

"Whoa, hold up there." Dean Bostwick marched over authoritatively. "Just what the hell do you think you're doing, Sullivan? Shouldn't you be looking at rocking chairs instead of my crime scene?" He smirked, straightening his expensive tie.

"I was hoping you'd grown up while I was gone," I told him. "But it looks like you're still going to need more time."

This generational warfare had been going on since he'd joined the force. I guess there was just something about me that irritated Bostwick, besides the fact that I was a woman. He'd been gunning for my job, jabbing me with snide insults, for years. Long before I retired, his childish routine had ceased to make anyone at the station even offer a slight smile toward me.

When he finally got promoted to chief of police, I congratulated him and even chipped in with the rest of the guys for a gift. But attending a party in his honor at Arezzo's—that was too much. I saw no reason to ever see the man again. And yet, there I was, staring into his angry eyes.

"I should have known you'd show up," Bostwick said. "You're hard to get rid of."

"Aren't you too old to be acting like a little boy?" I asked.

"Officer," Bostwick said to DeYoung, "please escort Mrs. Sullivan back to her vehicle." Then, turning to me, he added, "I assume you drove here. You can still do that, right? They didn't take away your license, did they?"

Before I could think of a snappy comeback, Nathan entered the room.

"Yo, Walker," one of the officers called out.

"Hey," Nathan waved in our direction. "You okay, Kathy?" He glared at Bostwick. "'Cause I'd just love an excuse to knock this smartass on his—"

"I'm fine, Nathan. Relax."

Bostwick was obviously insecure, always overcompensating for something none of us knew about. But underneath it all, he was a good cop. His performance at the academy had been outstanding and he deserved to be chief. However, because of his inadequacy issues, he struck out at everyone. And, like me, Nathan had just about had enough.

Bostwick snapped at Nathan. "You know better than anyone what the penalty for striking a police officer is. Just try something and I'll haul your ass into jail faster than you can—"

"Cut the macho crap," Nathan said. I could hear the other men in the room chuckling. "It isn't every day you get a murder in a place like this, is it? If I were you, Dean, I'd take advantage of two extra pairs of eyes belonging to seasoned, experienced officers who could make you look good. Know what I mean?"

"I don't need your help to make me look good."

"It would sure be a shame if word leaked out that you refused our professional expertise. Don't you think the Pierce family would consider it smart of you to consult with us?" I asked.

Bostwick threw up hands. "All right! I give up. But don't—"

Nathan turned to me. "Do you think he's actually going to tell us not to touch anything?" he asked sarcastically, making sure everyone in the room heard.

"Oh, he knows better than that," I said. "Right, Dean?"

Bostwick sucked in his bottom lip, obviously trying to keep himself from saying another word, and returned to the group of officers he had been speaking with before I arrived.

Nathan and I walked over to the body lying on the floor of the library. Circling several times, we finally stopped at the best vantage point to study the scene.

"I don't believe it," I whispered to Nathan. "That's Stacey Jordan. I just met her this morning. She worked for Randolph . . . at his gallery."

"Then what was she doing here?" he asked.

"She also worked part time with some expert, restoring this place. What a shame. She was such a sweet kid."

Stacey was lying on her side. Unlike the professional clothing she'd worn earlier, now she was dressed in a pair of jeans, old tennis shoes, and a sweatshirt that had some sort of sorority symbol on the front.

Nathan squatted down to get a closer look and I joined him. "She was hit from behind," he observed. "More than once I'd guess, from the severity of the wound on the back of her head."

"Which means she was either taken by surprise or running away from her attacker. And from the size and shape of the wound, it was a blunt object." I glanced around.

The large room was lined with bookcases on three sides. Every other one was filled with a collection of some sort. There were small porcelain vases, crystal figurines, music boxes, and half a dozen Faberge eggs—and also a lot of dead space where I guessed pieces were scheduled to be placed. The books had been covered with cloths. "It could have been something in this very room."

Nathan cocked his head, leaning closer, frustrated that he wasn't able to touch the body. "What do you make of those scratches on her arms?" he asked.

"Postmortem . . . they have to be, from the lack of blood surrounding them. I'd say whoever did this was an amateur and probably scratched poor Stacey while they were trying to move her. See the blood on the back of her shirt? She was hit from behind and would have fallen forward. Blood on the back of her shirt means she was turned over and dragged."

"I'm impressed," Nathan said. "So who do you think looks good for this?"

"Well, the most obvious suspects would be the two men who have access to the building: Randolph Pierce and the Frenchman . . . what was his name? Give me a minute . . . Antoine Rousseau. That's it."

"Seems logical," Nathan said. "Are you going to tell Bostwick?"

"Come on," I said, standing up and brushing off my jeans. "Do you really think he gives a damn what I think?" I looked over at the chief, and when he saw me, he turned his back.

"Most definitely not," Nathan said.

"Then I say we leave the police work to the police."

Nathan looked shocked. "So you're just going to walk away?"

"Hell no," I said. "We're going to solve this crime and make that smartass eat his words."

"Atta girl," Nathan said.

By the time I got home, the Internet was buzzing with news of Stacey Jordan's murder. I sat up reading postings from casual acquaintances to ex-boyfriends, all shocked to hear about her death. From what I could gather, her only sin had been falling behind on several student loans. She was well liked and didn't have any enemies . . . well, none that anyone knew about.

Grabbing a pad and pen, I made a list for the morning:

1. Call Randolph Pierce. Set up meeting and get Rousseau's number.
2. Meet Rousseau.
3. Find out who found the body and who called 9-1-1.

I knew all my questions wouldn't be answered tomorrow, but I was eager to get started. Although I wasn't the least bit sleepy, I forced myself to go to bed so that morning would come more quickly.

Chapter Nine

This time, I was up before anyone else in the house. I watched the local news on the small TV in the kitchen while making breakfast. Pierce Gallery wouldn't be open this early, and it was a good thing I didn't know Randolph's cell or home number, because I would have called him. So I fried bacon, waiting for the weather report to wrap up.

"Mother?" Lizzie stood at the door, looking like a snowball in her fluffy white robe. "What are you doing up so early?" She squinted at the clock near the stove. "The kids don't even get up for another hour."

When the anchorwoman with the bad hairdo came on the screen, I shushed my daughter. "I want to hear this."

"The body of twenty-eight-year-old Stacey Jordan, a recent graduate of the Minneapolis Institute of Arts, was found last night at the Pierce estate. Ms. Jordan suffered a fatal blow to the head and was pronounced dead on the scene. No murder weapon has been found. She had been assisting Antoine Rousseau, who was recently hired to oversee the restoration of the mansion. Mr. Rousseau, a French citizen, is a person of interest. The police are asking for your help in solving this senseless crime. If you have any information, please call the eight-hundred number at the bottom of your screen or go to our website." Then, as an aside, the woman added, "Some of you may remember that Marshall Pierce Senior also died in the estate under mysterious circumstances."

Before either one of us could speak, Lizzie's office phone rang. While she went to answer it, I put bread in the toaster, poured four glasses of orange juice, and started scrambling eggs before she returned, five minutes later.

"Well . . . you'll never guess who that was," she said, accepting the coffee mug I handed her.

"Who?"

"Randy."

"Randolph Pierce?" I asked. "What did he want?"

"He's at the police station; they brought him in for questioning."

I shrugged. "Standard procedure. After all, Stacey was found on his property. Is there a husband or boyfriend somewhere?"

"Not that I know of," Lizzie said.

Trying not to sound as though I was cross-examining her, I asked, "So why would he call you? It's not as if you two are close . . . or anything."

"He needs a lawyer."

"But you don't practice criminal law anymore. Didn't you tell him that?"

"Yes, Mother, I told him—several times. But he begged me to help, as a friend."

Friend? I studied her face, looking for some expression that would tell me more than her words or tone. There was no surprise around her eyes, no confusion tugging at the corners of her mouth. The last I knew, Lizzie couldn't stand Randolph. She'd disliked him when they were kids, and after more than twenty years, she still wasn't too fond of him. Granted, my daughter had always been compassionate and empathetic, but this was something else. She looked as though she'd been expecting his call.

"Did you know about Stacey before you went to bed last night?"

"How could I?" she asked defensively.

"Facebook, Twitter, e-mail, phone, local news websites—take your pick."

"All I knew was that you and Nathan ran off somewhere. After you left, I took a bath and went to bed. I didn't even hear you come in last night. Is that where you went? To the mansion?"

I nodded.

"Well, I better get dressed," she said, turning to leave.

"At least have some breakfast first," I said pulling out a chair for her at the table. "No waiting—it's all ready. It would be a shame to waste all this good food."

"You're right." Lizzie plopped down on the chair and started in on her eggs.

We had about twenty minutes alone before Cameron and Chloe got up. Then while the three of us ate, Lizzie ran around, getting dressed, looking for her briefcase and keys.

"Have a good day at school," she said, kissing each child on the head. "Grandma will take you and I'll pick you up."

I stood up, positioning myself for a hug. "Go get 'em, counselor."

The kids chattered in the backseat while I mentally went over the list I'd made the night before. Randolph Pierce was with detectives at that moment, so I'd have to speak with him later. Hopefully Antoine Rousseau had been released and I could get to him now.

After depositing Cam and Chloe safe and sound in front of their school, I called Nathan. Someone on his crew had to know where Rousseau was staying.

"He's out at the Lakeside Inn," Nathan told me. "My sources say he was hauled in and questioned late last night."

"Did they give him a polygraph?" I asked.

"The whole nine yards. He passed everything."

"But he could still be holding something back. I'm going out there to see him."

"Well you better hurry," Nathan said. "Last I

heard the man's real eager to leave town. Until this murder gets solved, the mansion is off limits, which means there's no reason for Rousseau to hang around."

"Did your sources also tell you where he was when Stacey was murdered?" I asked, driving toward the inn.

"The medical examiner estimates Stacey was killed somewhere between six and eight last night."

"And where was Antoine at that time?"

Nathan laughed. "For the life of me, I'll never understand what you women find so appealing about a Frenchman. He was out to dinner with Whitney Llewellyn."

"Our Whitney? The dispatcher?"

"One and the same. Dozens of people saw them together. Some of the guys at the station said he stopped by to pick her up after her shift. He has an ironclad alibi."

"Maybe I can catch him before he leaves," I said.

"You, Katherine Sullivan, are one stubborn lady."

"Come on Nathan, we both know that emotions are what drive someone to commit a crime and it has to be solved on a human level. When they invent a machine that can tell me what's in a man's eyes or how carefully he chooses his words, then maybe I'll leave things to the techies."

"No you won't."

"And *you* know me too well."

The inn was located near Lake Minnetonka, about twenty-five minutes west of Edina. Originally the country hotel was designed for honeymooners. It advertised hot tub rooms and plush suites with heart shaped beds. But when a large development company bought the acreage about ten years ago, their CEOs decided that "romantic" was corny and plowed everything under. Now an impressive "untraditional" five-story building stood in a clearing surrounded by koi ponds and walking trails.

In the lobby was a bank of house phones. I asked an operator to connect me to Antoine Rousseau's room and was surprised when he answered.

After introducing myself, I asked if I could come up and speak with him about Stacey Jordan.

"Such a beautiful girl," he said. "Such a pity."

"Yes," I agreed.

"But I have already spoken to the police, Madame. Please excuse me; I am very busy. I must pack my things and get to the airport. I have a three o'clock flight."

"I'll drive you myself," I offered, thinking that the trip would allow me extra time with the man.

"But it is nearly check-out time now. I am not sure if—"

"I'll talk to the desk clerk. You won't be charged for another day."

He'd run out of excuses and I was being ever so helpful.

"Five minutes," he said. "I can spare five minutes."

"Thank you."

After he gave me his room number, I went to the front desk to talk to the clerk. I still had my police ID, and even though it was out of date, no one ever looked at it that closely.

When he opened the door, he was holding a toiletry bag. After we made our introductions, he pointed to a chair by the desk and told me to sit. Stacey had been right about Rousseau's fastidiousness. Even in this casual moment, he was dressed impeccably, right down to his Gucci loafers. He'd even made the bed—or maybe hadn't slept in it the night before. One large, suede suitcase was packed and near the door. The smaller, matching piece was open, on top of a luggage rack. I could see several shirts neatly folded inside. Four shoes were on the bed, each wrapped in a monogrammed felt bag. A beautiful mahogany walking stick rested on a pillow.

He continued packing, and I wondered if he was intentionally being rude or just so involved in what he was doing that he'd already forgotten

I was there. So I began. "Thank you so much for seeing me, Mr. Rousseau. I appreciate it."

"Please, Madame, if you will be so kind as to tell me the exact reason for your visit . . ."

Immediately I could see that Antoine Rousseau was one of those people who imagined himself to be the most important person in any room he occupied. The only way to handle such a person was to punch away at their ego.

"I was the chief of police in Edina for years, Mr. Rousseau. This is my home; I love the people here. And Stacey Jordan was a friend of mine." Sometimes it's necessary to stretch the truth . . . just a little. "So I take her murder very personally."

He nodded. "I understand."

"When I learned that you had been taken in for questioning—"

His head snapped up and he glared at me. "Who told you about that?" he demanded.

I'd hit a nerve. "It was on the news this morning; by now everyone in town knows your name, Mr. Rousseau." I smiled. "Why, you're a regular celebrity."

He sat on the edge of the bed. "Oh no, no. I have a reputation. This is very bad. I cannot be associated in any way to the murder of an employee. Without my good name, I am nothing."

"What a shame. Maybe I could smooth things over a little . . . put in a good word. But I need to be more informed about your work at the mansion. You know, so I can answer questions from a more educated standpoint."

"Of course. Thank you so much. Merci, Mrs. Sullivan."

And we were off.

"I understand that you were hired by the board of directors, but who exactly did you deal with?"

"Randolph Pierce," he said.

"Do you know how Mr. Pierce became aware of you?"

Antoine stroked his chin, looking as if he was searching his memory. "I believe it was Mademoiselle Jordan who recommended me." Suddenly he shook his head. "I simply can't believe she is dead."

"Did you and Stacey work well together?"

"Oh, as well as can be expected."

Then I asked him, "How did you get along with Randolph?"

Antoine shrugged. "He was my employer. I think we both respected each other's work."

"Do you normally travel this far to consult?"

Excitedly, he said, "Oh, even in Paris there is talk of the great treasures hidden in the Pierce mansion. It would be a great coup to uncover hidden masterpieces."

Antoine Rousseau was suddenly not in any hurry. He genuinely seemed rattled by Stacey's death and answered all my questions sincerely.

But his main concern seemed to be the artwork he believed was hidden somewhere in the Pierce estate.

Everyone in town had grown up hearing stories about Marshall Senior. Some thought of him as a hero, aiding allied forces during World War II by producing helmets, tanks, and even airplane parts at Pierce Steel. Others considered him a ruthless tyrant who destroyed the environment, manipulated stock prices, and exploited his workers. But the one fact no one ever disputed was that the old man loved making money. Even though he'd inherited a fortune and made even more from government contracts, it wasn't enough. Rumor had it that he'd been smuggling stolen art out of Europe for years and hiding it in the walls of his mansion. Of course, no one in town believed the stories, except Rousseau, who seemed to think it was his duty to find and return the stolen pieces.

By the time we started for the airport, I was still not completely convinced of my passenger's innocence. When he spoke excitedly about master-pieces being hidden in the mansion, I thought that maybe—just maybe—he would have done anything to get at them, including murdering anyone who stood in his way. But to distract him, I asked about my other suspect: Randolph Pierce.

"He is like most men of his status," Rousseau said. "More money than sense."

"What did you think of him as an employer?" I asked. "Was he fair?"

"To me, yes. To those he thought of as his inferiors, no."

"Anything in particular you can remember?"

"I don't think he liked Mademoiselle Jordan very much. He was always shouting, threatening the poor girl."

"About what?" I asked.

"He accused her of being too nosey. He told her that if she gossiped about his family, he would fire her and make sure she never worked at another gallery. He had all sorts of connections in New York. He said he would have her black-listed."

"Did you tell the police this?"

"No, no. If what he said is true, he could also cause trouble for me. The art community is like a family, Madame. I would not be able to work in this country again. I have to protect myself. N'est-ce pas?"

"Yes," I told him, "you're right."

"Ahh, here's my gate." Antoine pointed.

I parked and stayed inside my vehicle while he unpacked the trunk. Then he came around to my side of the car. "It has been a real pleasure, Mrs. Sullivan. I hope we meet again."

I hated letting him go, but there was nothing I could do about it at that moment. "Oh, I'm sure we will, Mr. Rousseau. Have a good flight."

Chapter Ten

I was heading back to town, figuring I'd stop in at Nathan's office when my cell went off. Looking for a wide spot along the shoulder of the road, I pulled over.

"Mother! Where are you?"

"I'm out by the airport. Lizzie, what's the matter?"

"Randy's been picked up by the police. They're questioning him about Stacey's murder. Can you meet me for lunch? I need to talk. It's very important."

We agreed on Hopper's, a quiet little place, two exits east.

Realizing I had no idea where Lizzie was coming from when I got to the restaurant, I decided to go inside and grab a table. Even though there were only two cars in the parking lot, places filled up quickly at lunchtime.

I didn't recognize the hostess, and it was obvious she didn't know me. Her hair was pulled back into a ponytail, and she walked with such grace that I got the impression she had been a dancer once upon a time.

She started to seat me in the middle of the large room. Noticing a small table tucked in an alcove, I asked if I might sit there. She had to think about it for a moment, even though there was only one other table occupied in the whole place. But I got it and promptly ordered a glass of Riesling while I waited for Lizzie.

I was thinking of ordering an appetizer when my daughter came rushing through the door. She talked to the hostess, who pointed at me. Then Lizzie hurried over.

"Sorry I'm late. Have you been waiting long?" Her cheeks were pink and she seemed out of breath as she hooked her tote over the back of a chair. "This has been one hell of a day. That wine looks good. Think I'll have to join you." Finally she sat down.

"What's going on? Are you okay?"

"Oh, Mother," she said in a defeated tone. "My client is *still* being detained for questioning and is probably going to be arrested and charged with murder. I'm a terrible lawyer. I should never have agreed to do this. I feel awful."

"Well, let's get you that wine and, calmly, after you've decompressed, tell me what's got you so upset. Because I know you've been in this situation countless times before. I also know you're an excellent lawyer."

While she gave the waitress her drink order, I studied Lizzie. Something was going on. "Are you ladies ready to order lunch now? Or should I come back later?"

Hoping to keep interruptions at a minimum, I told her we were ready. Lizzie looked at the menu bewildered, so I took charge. "We'll both have the Cobb salad."

After our waitress left, a party of five women walked in, then two businessmen. As Hopper's started to fill up, I waited patiently for my daughter to start explaining the real reason we were there.

I'd mastered the art of silence long ago. The trick is in the steady stare and noncombative demeanor. I can make any person sitting across from me spill their guts in under five minutes.

"I know what you're doing, Mother," she finally said.

"So talk to me. Start at the beginning."

She twisted a strand of hair around the index finger of her left hand. It was a habit she'd developed the first day of school, brought on by anxiety. "When I got to the police station, they had Randy in an interrogation room. He'd been there about an hour. Never once did it cross his mind that he might be a murder suspect. He cooperated and answered every question as thoroughly as he could. But after twenty minutes or so, the cops got aggressive. That's when he shut down and refused to take a lie detector test or be swabbed for a DNA sample. Which made him look more suspicious."

I nodded.

"His family has a battalion of lawyers, but he

doesn't really know any of them . . . so he asked for me."

"Where was Randolph last night? Does he have an alibi? Or is that confidential information between an attorney and her client?"

"You're doing it again, Mother," Lizzie whispered. "After all these years, I think it's second nature now. You can't help interrogating everyone—including your own daughter."

She was right. I wasn't chief of police anymore; I was a private citizen. Just a mother out with her daughter, having a nice peaceful lunch. Or at least I was trying to.

Our waitress suddenly appeared, balancing a large salad bowl in each hand. By the time she added fresh ground pepper, filled the water glasses, and asked if we needed anything else, we were distracted. After she left, we busied ourselves buttering the warm bread, drizzling dressing, and the moment to apologize had passed.

"The reason I needed to see you, Mother, is to offer you a job as private investigator for the defense. Use some of your skills to my benefit— for a change."

I sat there with a mouth full of tomatoes and a face full of surprise.

When she saw me like that, Lizzie laughed. "And, as such, you'll be privy to everything I know. That has to please you, right?"

I took a gulp of water. "Yes, it does. But before

I agree to anything, tell me about your personal involvement with Randolph. Am I wrong in thinking there's something going on between you two?"

She shook her head, slowly. "I didn't think I could hide it from you much longer."

"Were you corresponding with him all the time he was in New York? While you were married?"

"No. I never saw him after graduation . . . until a few months ago. Honest. But I've had a crush on him for years. Don't tell me you didn't know that."

"You never said anything about it."

"Still."

I couldn't help but smile. "I had my suspicions. Do you think your father knew?"

She looked mortified. "God, no. I would have died."

"And you never told Randolph? Or had a girlfriend drop a hint?"

"What was the use? My parents were cops. His were millionaires; they owned a mansion. Randolph had been around the world by the time he was eighteen. Why would someone like him look at me twice? That's how my brain worked back then. I was just a dumb kid."

"And now he's here and single. You're here and divorced. So you decided to just go for it?"

"Not exactly," Lizzie said, picking at her salad. "I went to the gallery one day; I was curious. He was there and we ended up going out for a drink. That's when he confessed he'd had a crush on me back in high school, too. Isn't that funny? Randolph Pierce—the richest boy in town—liked me."

"Funny ha-ha or funny strange?"

"Come on, you know what I mean."

"Sorry."

"Anyway, he was afraid of what his parents would say. Just think, all that time we could have been dating. No telling where it might have led. Maybe I would have never married Tom."

"But you did. And you have two wonderful kids to show for it."

Lizzie smiled at my comment and went on. "We've been seeing each other ever since. He's really changed, Mother. If you give him a chance, you'll see how wonderful he is." Her face lit up.

"Well, had I known any of this sooner, I would have advised you to not represent him. Having a romantic attachment to a client usually ends up badly."

"I know," she said.

"And against my better judgment, I'll help you. Remember I'm doing this to find Stacey's killer."

"And get Randolph out of jail, too, right?" Lizzie asked.

"Well . . . that will happen when I figure all this out."

"Whatever the reason, we're both grateful."

Chapter Eleven

Lizzie called to set up my meeting with Randolph Pierce. We celebrated our working arrangement with coffee and strudel. Then she headed back to the office and I drove to the jail on West Fiftieth Street. It was a different man who sat there than the one I'd seen in the gallery. Randolph Pierce was frightened. When we were finally alone, he looked so relieved I thought he might cry.

"Thank God you're here, Mrs. Sullivan. You've got to tell them I didn't kill Stacey." He pounded his fist on the table between us. "Why in the world would I?"

"Calm down, Randolph. I know you're upset but I've never come across a suspect who didn't scream he was innocent. So turn the hysterics down a notch."

He took a deep, cleansing breath. "I'll try."

"Before we go any further I need you to promise that everything you're going to tell me is the truth. I can't help you if you lie."

He nodded.

To make good and sure I had his full attention, I started off strong. "I know about you and Lizzie. I'm not sure how I feel about your relationship with my daughter, but my feelings aren't relevant here. I just wanted to get that out so we don't waste time skirting around the issue."

"I can see how you'd be upset, but I love Lizzie. I have for years. Believe me, I would never have gotten her involved in all this mess if I had anywhere else to turn. Your daughter is a wonderful woman. I'd never hurt her, Mrs. Sullivan."

It was the first time I'd ever had a glimpse into Randolph Pierce's heart. But human nature being what it was, I didn't count on there being a second look.

"I spoke with Antoine Rousseau this morning after he'd been questioned. He was released because, unlike you, he had an alibi. Randolph, I need you to tell me where you were the night Stacey was killed."

"At home, just hanging out. I told the cops a hundred times that there was no one to vouch for me. I was alone."

"Tell me exactly what you did." I took a small pad and pen out of my purse and started making notes. "Every little detail you can remember."

"I brought home a pizza and ate it while the news was on."

"Where did you get the pizza from? Which channel were you watching? The tiniest thing can end up being important."

He looked frustrated but began again. "I picked up a pizza at Red's—thin crust, sausage, mushrooms, and extra cheese. I took it home and turned on the six o'clock news. After the pizza was gone and the news was over, I caught up on a few episodes of *Mad Men*. Before going to bed, I looked through the mail. And that was it."

"I can go to Red's and see if anyone remembers you. There should be a record of your order, a receipt. I'll need plots of the *Mad Men* episodes you watched. Hopefully, I can find something that will prove you were alone at home the whole night."

"The sooner, the better. Anything so I don't have to stay in this hole another minute longer."

"Come on," I laughed. "This isn't exactly some overcrowded prison in Calcutta. From what I can see, there are three of you here, all in your own clean, modern cell. Relax." I hated to admit it, but I was enjoying seeing a Pierce squirm.

He rolled his eyes. "I'm just not used to being treated this way."

I knew he couldn't shake off a lifetime of arrogance in one day and leaned in closer so he wouldn't miss anything I was going to say. "Knock off that attitude . . . even if you have to fake it. All you're doing is alienating everyone around you. And take that polygraph—unless you think you won't pass."

"I'll pass."

"Good." At least I'd gotten that far with him. "Now, when I spoke with Antoine, he told me you argued with Stacey. He said everyone in the room heard. What was that all about?"

Randolph ran his fingers through his hair. "Look, Stacey was a hard worker but she was intrusive—in your face, you know? Always going where she didn't belong. I was constantly telling her to stop nosing around and just do her job. But as soon as she thought I was gone, she'd ask the workers or Rousseau, anyone she could find, about me and my family. How much were we worth, how had my grandfather died, on and on— she was relentless. I finally had enough. I lost it that day and told her that if she didn't mind her own business, I'd have to let her go."

"How did she react?"

"She got angry. She threatened to go to the authorities," he said.

"Just because you yelled at her?"

"She'd heard the stories . . . like everyone in this town has. You know, about Grandfather buying stolen art from the Nazis."

"Wasn't there supposed to be a Klimt? I remember because when I studied art, I used to imagine that piece being at Buckhorn instead of hanging in some museum thousands of miles away. It was a nice fantasy." I smirked. "But I never believed a word of it."

Randolph put his head down, trying to hide his lips from the security camera on the wall. "Well, believe it, Mrs. Sullivan. The Klimt is there."

Chapter Twelve

I couldn't think straight after Randolph told me about the masterpiece. It was like suddenly learning Santa Claus was real and living in the attic. Of course I wanted proof, to see it with my own eyes. But I was torn between the realist and the artist in me.

The creative part of my psyche yearned to touch the canvas, hold it close, and get lost in each brushstroke. But the cop in me was outraged and wanted to return the painting to Austria where it belonged. Was there actually a Klimt hidden in the walls of an old mansion in Minnesota? The idea seemed too farfetched for either part of me to believe.

Before going home, I dropped in at my old station to see if there had been any new developments in their investigation. Bostwick had left for the day and even the cops who had been hired after my retirement disliked their chief so much they were eager to help me. Word had come down that I had dared to challenge their boss. Knowing how cops thought, I wouldn't be surprised if they were taking bets in the back room to see who would solve the case first.

DeYoung was on duty and laid out the facts. The murder weapon had still not been found. It would take a few more days until results came in from prints taken at the scene. They'd already started the laborious task of fingerprinting all the workers at the mansion. But there had been so many construction crews in and out over the past six months that a few would surely slip through the cracks. An autopsy was being performed; the medical examiner's report had not come in yet. There wasn't one new piece of evidence for me to work with.

But the court of public opinion doesn't need hard-core evidence; it operates on gut feelings. Randolph Pierce had not only been uncooperative but flaunted his contempt for the police. Most of the men on duty had gone to school with him, but he never acknowledged having known any of them. He was beyond arrogant, they said—he was mean. And even though none of them would say it out loud, they were already thinking of him as guilty.

I needed to put my feet up and review what I'd learned so far, which wasn't much. Making sure to thank everyone, I turned to leave. My hand was on the door and as I started to pull it open, someone on the other side pushed with such force I almost got smacked in the face.

A muscular, larger-than-life male shoved his way inside. I don't think he was even aware I was in the room. From a thick gold chain wrapped tightly around his thick neck hung a gold cross. He wore a sweatshirt two sizes too small, obviously to show off his muscles. Spandex bike shorts, sandals, and a few tattoos completed his ensemble. And I use the term very loosely. His hair was long, pulled into a stringy ponytail that had been threaded through the back of a baseball cap. After bursting into the room, he stopped, stood at attention, and held the door open. DeYoung stared at the man with a bemused look on his face, which I returned.

We all waited to see what was next.

After a minute, in walked a tiny, much older woman. At first I didn't recognize her. Nothing about her stature or face looked familiar. It was her outfit that triggered a memory. She was wearing it at an awards show when a picture had been snapped, ending up in our local paper. That had to have been at least thirty years ago.

Her wrinkled face had several layers of makeup, some of it cracking across her forehead. Red circles of blush made her skin look even paler. I wondered if she was still wearing the same shade of Chanel red lipstick that had been her trademark. The whole effect made her look like a bizarre kewpie doll.

She wore a full-length silver, sequined gown— too large for her and cut far too low. A turban made of the same fabric was wrapped tightly around her head. Stray wisps of black hair stuck out around her ears. Her mink coat looked moth eaten. The sight of her made me feel sad and embarrassed at the same time.

Then she spoke. "I believe you're holding my nephew here. I'm Jacqueline Bannister-Pierce, his aunt. I'll assume full responsibility for him. Are there some papers I need to sign?"

The behemoth walked over to stand by her side, all the while chomping on a thick wad of gum. "And I'm Henry—"

"Shut up, Hank," Jackie snapped. Then to DeYoung, she said, "Mr. Slater is a close friend."

"And her bodyguard." He smiled.

I couldn't move. It was all so entertaining.

"I'm sorry," the desk sergeant said, "but Mr. Pierce isn't going anywhere."

"Look, I've just flown all the way from Las Vegas. Do you know how far that is?"

"Yes ma'am, I've been to Las Vegas. Spent five days at Caesar's Palace last vacation."

Jackie didn't miss a beat. "Well good for you. Now just tell me how much it will cost to get Randolph out of here."

"Considering the fact that the charge is murder and he's a flight risk, there is no bail—that is, when he's charged with murder. Right now he's being held for questioning."

Her wrinkled face sagged. "I'll be speaking

to my lawyer about that tomorrow. But for now may I see him?"

"Wait over there." He pointed to a wooden bench.

Jackie looked mortified. "Isn't there a private lounge where I can wait?"

As soon as the show was over, I left.

I'd needed to turn my phone off at the jail and switched it back on as I walked to the car. There were three messages:

1. "Mother, I have to take Cam to his speech therapist and Chloe has soccer practice. We'll grab something afterwards. So you're on your own for dinner. There's plenty in the fridge. See you."
2. "It's me again. I have to hear everything that happened at the jail with Randy. We shouldn't be very late. Love you."
3. "Hey, it's Nathan. What's going on? I need details, woman."

I waited until I had gotten settled in the kitchen with a ham sandwich in front of me before returning Nathan's call.

There wasn't much to tell. I started from the beginning, reviewing my conversations with Antoine and Randolph. "There wasn't anything new at the station either. Any suggestions?"

"Did you ever find out who made the nine-one-one call? Maybe it's the same person who found Stacey's body."

"No one has a clue."

"Why don't you meet me for lunch tomorrow at the diner, around one? I'll bring my crew. They're an odd bunch, but between the six of us, we'll be able to come up with the name of the caller."

"I've never thought of you as having a 'crew.' It seems strange."

"Good strange or bad strange?" he asked.

"I'll let you know tomorrow."

Chapter Thirteen

The Twelfth Street Diner wasn't on Twelfth Street and had never been on Twelfth Street. The original owner, Benny Angelo, had moved to Minnesota from Brooklyn with his wife, five kids, and a handful of Mama Rose's recipes. He claimed it was to give his family a better quality of life and named the place in honor of his old neighborhood so he'd never forget where he came from.

Whenever my dad had a craving for Benny's three-bean chili, which always seemed to come in the middle of the night, he'd get us out of bed and we'd drive out to the diner. I can't remember how many times I sent poor Sully out there for a meatloaf sandwich when I was pregnant. It was the scene of Lizzie's first date. Over the years, going to the Twelfth became a tradition in our family. But I hadn't been there since a Yuppie couple from Connecticut bought it and Benny moved to Florida. It was nice they kept the name.

It still smelled the same: greasy burgers and coffee. As I walked across the worn, wooden floor, it creaked and I was happy to see nothing had changed. The old jukebox flashed in the corner, red vinyl still covered stools at the counter, but the ancient cash register had been replaced with a computer station. I guess you can't hold back progress completely. A tall man with an apron wrapped around his waist handed me a menu and asked if I preferred a table or a booth.

"I'm meeting someone," I told him as I surveyed the room.

"Hey, Kathy." Nathan waved to get my attention. He's the only person who ever called me Kathy . . . and I liked it.

"There he is," I told the host.

Nathan stood up. "Squeeze in and I'll make the intros."

The booth was extra long and I slid across the red vinyl toward a tough-looking middle-aged woman. Nathan slid in next to me.

"That heathen over there," he pointed to a muscular man, hunkered over what looked to be a triple-decker burger surrounded by a mountain of fries, "is Brock. The first time I ran into this monster, he was hauling some guy twice his size out of a club. As far as I can tell, he's a cross between a rock and a brick."

Brock grabbed a napkin and wiped his right hand clean then extended it across the table toward me. "So now, I'm Brock. Nice to meet you, Mrs. Sullivan. Didn't mean to start without you but I ain't eaten in a few hours." I couldn't tell if he was smiling at me, his beard was so thick, matching all the hair on his head. He looked like a bear.

I expected a painful grip, but Brock shook my hand gently. "Nice to meet you. And please," I looked around the table, "all of you, call me Katherine."

Everyone nodded.

Nathan continued. "You may have guessed, Brock's our muscle. Don't let the big guy scare you; he's a real pussycat."

Everyone at the table laughed—except Brock, who scowled and continued eating.

"I'm E.T.," the man across from me said. Around thirty years old, he was almost Brock's opposite: thin, focused, and very serious. Wispy light brown hair hung to his shoulders. He seemed uncomfortable and just nodded a hello. A bottle of mineral water sat in front of him, obviously bought elsewhere. His shoulders were narrow, and under his camouflage jacket, he wore a Green Peace T-shirt.

"Did Nathan give you that name?" I asked.

"Yeah, he caught me once—okay twice—eating some of the candy he keeps on his desk."

Everyone at the table groaned.

"Get real," Nathan said. "You're the reason I had to start hiding the stuff."

"You shouldn't even be eating sweets at your age," E.T. told Nathan.

Nathan ignored E.T.'s comment. "This guy's

our expert in nonlethal weaponry and martial arts. He installs alarms in private homes. He's the best. In and out, without a trace."

"I'm impressed," I said.

The young woman next to E.T. spoke up. "Hi, I'm Polly. That's not my real name, of course. I made this polygraph machine and brought it in to my interview with Nathan—"

"—and blew me away," Nathan said. "Never saw anything like it."

"So Polly it is."

She shrugged. Polly was the youngest in the group, twenty-something and cute. Through the long straight bangs that covered her forehead, I could see an eyebrow had been pierced. Dozens of thin bracelets were stacked along her arms and on each thumb she wore a silver ring.

"Polly's our electronics, computer, and surveillance expert. Her videos have gone viral; she's exposed animal abuse carried on by some of the major food and cosmetics corporations in the country."

"Give me an animal or computer anytime," she said. "People suck, ya know what I mean?"

"I'm sorry to say I do."

"And last but not least is Rosie," Nathan said and nodded to the woman sitting next to me.

I turned to get a good look at her. "Hi."

"A pleasure." She gave me a quick smile.

Rosie looked just like the woman in the World

War Two poster: Rosie the Riveter. This time I could see why Nathan had chosen her name. She gave off an aura of competence and strength. Fifty-something, she sported a short haircut. She'd rolled the sleeves of her plaid shirt up exposing tattoos on each arm. With no jewelry, no piercings, Rosie was obviously the no-nonsense type.

"Rosie had to leave Chicago in a hurry and was looking for work," Nathan said.

"Got mixed up with some wise guys, my ex included." She ran her large hands through the sides of her pompadour. "He was connected—know what I mean? On our honeymoon, get this, he takes me out on my first job. Breaking into some McMansion on Lake Shore Drive. What an idiot." She nudged me and laughed. "Him an' his buddies didn't know what the hell they was doin'. We got away with one thousand lousy bucks, split four ways. Can you believe it?"

"Rosie's a master locksmith and B and E expert," Nathan said.

"Almost makes me sound respectable, don't he?" she asked and nudged me again.

"He does have a way with words," I told her.

While a waitress took our order, I looked around the table. What a bunch, I thought, realizing I liked every one of them.

Nathan continued when we were alone again.

"Before we go any further, I want to say something about Katherine . . . and her husband, Sully," he told the group. I couldn't imagine what was coming next. "No one was used to seeing a black face on the force, back in the day. You young folks can't even imagine the racial slurs, the tension. More than once, I wanted to give up. But then Sully insisted we be partners and things started to change for me. I became more accepted on the job, and Kathy, Sully, my wife and I, we all became like family. They both always had my back. We started going to each other's homes for dinner. Our kids played together . . ."

"Come on, Nathan, you and Terry were always there for us, too. You make Sully and me sound like saints."

"No, Kathy, you guys went way beyond the definition of friends. And I'll never forget your kindness . . . never."

I was overwhelmed; all I could do was pat his hand.

After a short moment of uncomfortable silence, Brock spoke up. "If the boss says you're okay, that's good enough for us."

"Yeah, he laid everything out before you got here," Rosie added. "We got you covered. Not to worry."

"Even though their system is ancient out there at the manse, I'm sure I can come up with something," Polly said. "Nothing's ever lost; it just bounces around out in the ozone until someone finds it."

"You're all so . . . remarkable," I stammered. "I don't know how to thank you."

"No, we're the ones who should be thankin' you," Rosie said. "Solvin' a murder! This is gonna be great!"

Chapter Fourteen

The Pierce Art Gallery was on my way home. With Randolph in jail, I assumed it would be closed and had no intention of stopping . . . until I saw them. Jacqueline Pierce, Hank, and Antoine were all standing out front, huddled close together in conversation. I had to find out what was going on and parked in the middle of the block.

I'd hoped they'd all be surprised to see me— especially Antoine. But when I walked up to the group, they just seemed annoyed by my presence.

"Mrs. Sullivan," Antoine began. "What are you doing here?"

"I was going to ask you the same thing, Mr. Rousseau. Yesterday when you had me drop you off at the airport, I assumed you were leaving town."

"Haven't you ever made people think you're doing one thing and then do another?" Hank said smugly. He never made eye contact with me, just kept staring through the gallery window. "Didn't anyone ever tell you not to believe anything you see and half of what you hear?"

I hated that Hank was making me feel dumb. He was obviously smarter, or much more cunning, than he let on.

"And since we're all so very curious about each other, might I ask why you're here?" Jackie turned to face me. "You do seem to pop up in the most unusual places. Why, I even saw you last night at the police station."

I knew she was baiting me. But as she stood there in her pink silk dress, frayed along the hem, I had a hard time taking her seriously. Her bony legs were wrapped in baggy hose. Even though it was a warm afternoon, she still wore the same fur coat. Several strands of pearls draped across her chest. A large opal ring was on her index finger and a clashing, oversized bracelet with multicolored jewels dangled on her left wrist. Her turban had been replaced with a pink feather. She was hoping her tone would intimidate me, but it only made me feel sorry for her.

"You were there on business, Ms. Pierce; it wasn't the right time to socialize."

"It's always party time," Hank laughed.

Antoine rolled his eyes and pursed his lips. He was stylish in a navy suit and yellow cravat. "As my fear subsided, I realized I couldn't leave without completing my work at the estate. And of course, Mademoiselle Jordan's murder has been weighing heavily on my heart. Such an intelligent woman, a true connoisseur of the arts. To be cut down in her prime like that . . . horrible."

"I understand that your daughter, Elizabeth, is

representing my nephew." Jackie said. "I was telling Mr. Rousseau that I will do everything in my power to make Randolph seek a more acceptable attorney. As sweet as she is, and no matter how much affection my nephew has for her, Elizabeth represents . . . poor people. You know the kind I'm talking about." She looked to the men for validation. "I've heard all the stories. How on earth could that kind of a lawyer handle a murder case?"

I counted to three before I spoke. As hard as I was trying not to react, this crazy woman was getting to me. "Maybe you're not aware, Jackie, but Elizabeth practiced criminal law for years before becoming a children's advocate."

Continuing as if she hadn't heard a word I'd said, Jackie tilted her nose further up in the air. "And you, Mrs. Sullivan, you're retired now. Aren't you a bit too old to be running around playing detective? We're two of a kind, you and I," she cackled. "We've both seen better days, haven't we?"

I ignored her and looked at Antoine. "I'm afraid the mansion is a crime scene and you won't be able to go inside until the police finish gathering all their evidence. But you knew that the other day, didn't you?"

He shoved one hand deep into a pocket and with his other, waved his walking stick dramatically. "Of course, but I thought that . . . maybe . . . if I presented my case before Mrs. Bannister-Pierce, that she might . . . be able to persuade the authorities to let me enter."

"Mrs. Bannister-Pierce is not the owner of the estate." I really enjoyed saying that. And I continued, ignoring the woman who glared up at me. "Her father's will specifically stated that she is forbidden to have anything to do with Buckhorn manor—now or in the future."

Antoine looked deflated. "I was unaware of the situation,"

"My, my, you're just a wealth of knowledge, aren't you?" Jackie said. I could see red lipstick smeared across her front teeth as she growled at me. "For the life of me, I don't understand how you would know so much about the will. It's not as if you're a member of my family."

"It was my job to know about the people in this town. And I was good at my job." I growled right back at her.

Hank looked at his Rolex. "Hey, babe," he said to Jackie. "Are we done here? I have some business to take care of."

"I'd say we definitely are," she said and put her arm through his. Then the two of them walked away.

Antoine looked unsure how to proceed and smiled weakly at me. "If I may call you, Madame, to find out when I may enter the—"

"I suggest you contact the police department yourself, Mr. Rousseau. And please don't tell me where you're staying this time because I'm not sure I'd believe you."

"As you wish."

"Yes," I smiled, "that's exactly as I wish."

It had never mattered to me if I got in the last word. But I had to confess I felt good about the way I'd handled those three. And I laughed part of the way home. The other part was spent wondering why they'd been outside the gallery in the first place. Had Randolph been keeping his aunt updated about the renovations or had she just found out?

Lizzie's car was in the driveway. Checking my watch, I realized it was time for everyone to be home. A few miles back, I'd passed a Mexican restaurant and a sudden craving for guacamole hit me.

"Grandma's home!" I shouted as I walked through the door. "Come adore me!"

Cam walked out of his room, smiling. "You look very happy today," he said.

"Well I'm looking at you." I hugged him. "How's my guy?"

"Lewis asked me to come over to his house for dinner. His mom's making mac and cheese."

"That sounds like fun. And you love mac and cheese, right?"

"His brother, Jeff, will be there. He goes to college. I don't know him."

"Well now's your chance."

"What if he doesn't like me? I'm afraid to go, Grammy."

He looked up at me and I wanted to whisk him off to a place where he'd never be afraid or hurt. I gently brushed his cheek. "You know what sounds good?" Before he could answer I said, "Tacos!"

"I like chicken ones," he said. "The soft kind."

"I know you do. So let's go get some. Just you, me, Chloe, and Mom. You can meet Lewis's brother another time—when you're ready."

He mulled the idea over. "That sounds better. I'll go finish my homework."

I kissed the top of his head and watched him walk back to his room.

After searching the house, I found Lizzie in her office.

"Hi, Mother. How was your day?"

"You first," I said.

"I'll let you know when it's over. I've got a couple more calls to make. Haven't even had time to think about dinner. Could you—"

"—How about I take everyone to that cute Mexican place near the park? My treat. And you can't say no, 'cause I just promised Cam some tacos."

"Sounds great. Chloe's in her room, if you want

to tell her. I should be finished in here by six."
Her phone rang as I went in search of Chloe.

There was no telling what kind of mood my granddaughter would be in, so I knocked cautiously on her door.

"What?" she shouted.

"It's your grandmother. Can I come in?"

"I guess so."

She seemed frustrated that I was invading her privacy.

"Hey, Chloe girl, whatcha up to?" I asked as I sat on the edge of her bed.

She was spread out on top of the plush beige carpet. Her legs were crossed in front of her; her back against the wall. "Not much."

Lizzie, Tom, and I had decorated the room when Chloe was nine. She'd been into stars, moons, and rainbows then. Her ceiling was painted navy blue with constellations stenciled across it. Her walls were a pale blue. I'd spent a whole week painting the sun that covered the entire wall behind her bed. And another two days working on the rainbow. Beside her bed, on a nightstand painted blue to match the walls, was a lamp I'd found in a museum shop. The base was a pewter crescent moon and the silver shade had star-shaped punches scattered across it.

But four years are an eternity in a little girl's life and changes had taken place, not only in the bedroom but inside the girl herself. Pictures of Disney princesses and cartoon characters were gone. They'd all been replaced by her current loves: boy bands, pieces of poetry, and fashion. I was glad to see my granddaughter was a normal, healthy teenager.

"Did I ever tell you about the first concert I went to?" Chloe couldn't have cared less, but I continued. "The Rolling Stones were on tour and I drove down to Chicago with my girlfriend to see them. Seven very long hours in that car. We had just enough money for gas and snacks. And we had to drive back home after it was over because we couldn't afford a motel." I stopped, waiting for some reaction. But there was none.

"We thought we were so cool. But when they finally came on stage and I saw Mick, right there in front of me, I lost it. I couldn't stop screaming. You've seen those girls in movies carrying on and fainting. Well, sorry to say, I was one of them. But I couldn't stop myself. I cried all the way through the first two songs. It was one of the best nights of my life."

"Sounds great," she said, not bothering to look at me.

I pointed to a poster. "So, have you seen One Direction live?"

"You know who they are?" she asked, finally interested.

"Hey, I know things."

Suddenly, unable to control her enthusiasm, Chloe gushed. "Jennifer thinks Harry is the cutest but I like Liam. He's gorg. I know all their songs by heart. Mom says she'll take us if they ever come here. But if she can't, Dad said he'll take us, if he's in town. That would be so a . . . maz . . . ing."

When she ran out of air, we just sat there and smiled at each other.

"You'll have a great time," I said. "And I want to hear every detail."

Then she remembered she was angry with me and looked down at her feet. "Okay."

"Have you been writing in your journal?" I asked.

"A little."

"Can I see?"

She reached under the pillow next to her and I realized she'd been writing in it when I walked in.

"How about if you read to me? Please?"

"Isn't this supposed to be private? For my eyes only?"

"It's not a diary, sweetie. Come on—share."

Chloe cleared her throat and started to read. "Grandma really pisses me off." Then she looked up for a reaction.

"I'm not going to get mad at anything you write, Chloe."

She looked back down at the book and read

some more. "I guess old people don't remember things. Maybe she never had a BFF so she can't understand. I hope when I'm old like her, I'll be nice to kids. It's crappy being a kid, all the time having to do what everyone tells you. When I'm grown-up, I'll listen real good." She slammed the book shut and looked at me, defiantly.

"Ouch, you're the second person today to tell me I'm old. And I do remember my BFF when I was your age was Ingrid Stanberry. She moved to Dallas when I was eleven. Then there was Mattie Wilson. And after her it was Lorie Peterson. Then there was Grandpa . . ."

"But now that he's . . . gone?"

"I guess it's Nathan—Mr. Walker."

"He's nice." Her face started to soften. "Mom says he was a hunk."

I nodded. "And you're right about being a kid; it was lousy. Rules, everyone always telling me what to do. I hated it. But then, all of a sudden, BAM, I was on my own. Before you know it, you will be too. And you'll look around and no one will care what you do. Everyone will be taking care of their kids or husbands or jobs. Every now and then, I look around and wish my mother was still around to tell me what to do."

"Really?" She thought about that for a moment.

Having made a little headway, I decided to get out while the getting was good.

"I'm taking everyone out for tacos. Your mom will be ready around six. Meet you in the living room."

As I opened her door she said, in her little girl voice, "Love you, Gram."

"Love you, too, Chloe girl."

Chapter Fifteen

Dos Hermanos was crowded and lively. The inside was designed to look like a village somewhere in Acapulco. A mariachi band strolled from table to table, trying to be heard above the baby crying near the door. Small children ran back and forth playing tag while their parents gulped down margaritas. If there had been any indication out front that this was a "family friendly" restaurant, I would have suggested somewhere else. But we were hungry and there was immediate seating.

A waiter came rushing over, holding a sizzling pan of beef and peppers. "Is the table over there, okay?" He motioned with his head.

I told him it was fine.

With his free hand, he grabbed four menus and handed them to us. "I'll send a waiter over to take your order."

Cameron sank down in his seat and I hoped all the commotion wasn't upsetting him. Chloe couldn't take her eyes off the machine in the middle of the room that was making taco chips. Lizzie and I read through the menu.

A teenager dressed in a brightly colored tropical shirt came over with a basket of chips and a bowl of salsa. He carefully set them down in the middle of our table, smiled, and introduced himself as Ruiz. The kids ordered tacos; Lizzie and I decided to share an order of fajitas. During the five minutes it took, he never stopped smiling or saying, "Bueno, bueno." Then, gathering the menus, he left promising to return quickly with our drinks.

It was impossible to have a conversation with all the activity around us, so we dipped our chips in salsa and crunched away until the food arrived.

Suddenly, as if everyone in the place except us heard a distant whistle, they started to leave. First the family with the baby, then kids, some screaming they wanted to stay, others running to be the first out the door. Even the mariachis took a break. The air in the large room seemed calmer, lighter. And miraculously, I could not only hear myself think but make out what Lizzie was saying. Before we were able to really talk, however, our food was ready.

Two waiters covered our table with colorful plates and for a while we were all so busy eating that no one spoke. The only sound surrounding us was easy listening music coming from the speakers in the corners. I could feel myself relaxing while I loaded up a tortilla. Cameron rocked back and forth as he happily ate his chicken taco and Chloe seemed more content than I'd seen her in days. Between bites, Lizzie asked me about my day.

Even the kids seemed interested and listened intently while I told them about Nathan's crew. Cam said that Brock sounded like the hulk and Chloe seemed curious about Polly. Both of them thought it was funny how Nathan had given each member a nickname and the discussion got sidetracked when they started giving names to each other. When there was finally an opening, I mentioned that I'd run into Antoine, Jackie, and Hank in front of the gallery.

Lizzie dropped her fork. "How dare that old hag criticize me," she said when I repeated Jackie's comments about Randolph needing a different lawyer. "I've been on the phone all day and at the courthouse and jail on Randy's behalf. I know more about criminal law than anyone in this town."

"She's crazy; everybody knows that. Why are you so upset?" I asked.

"It doesn't look good, Mother. Randy was seen arguing with Stacey. He threatened to fire her in front of the workers. He'd been complaining about her for days. His prints are everywhere."

I dabbed my mouth with a napkin. "Of course they are. He's been in and out of that place his whole life."

Lizzie wanted to make sure the kids weren't going to hear the next part of our conversation and sent them over to the chip machine to refill our basket. When they were out of earshot, she said, "I'm afraid the ME will find Randy's skin under Stacey's nails."

This was news to me. "Why would he?" I asked.

"Earlier that day, Randy found Stacey snooping around where she didn't belong. He grabbed her arm, and she pushed him away. He noticed a few marks she'd left with those long nails of hers. That's all they need to lock him away forever."

"But when they examined him after they brought him in, they checked for bruises or marks," I said. "It's standard procedure. Have you seen the report yet?"

"It's too early."

"Have you encouraged him to take the polygraph? That would help a lot."

"I've tried but he still refuses."

"Any word on the murder weapon?" I asked her.

Lizzie twisted a strand of hair between her fingers. "Maybe Nathan's crew can work on that one."

"I'll ask him. Between the four of them, I'd think they can do anything."

"Let's hope so."

Dinner was delicious, but by the time we finished our flan, my mind had started trying to sort through Randolph's predicament again. I needed some time alone. After dropping everyone off at the house, I went for a drive to try to get it all straight.

Sully used to scold me that I thought everything to death. He was always encouraging me to rely more on my instincts, which consistently produced better results than all the programs our techies used. I just needed some quiet time to sort through all that had happened over the past three days.

Opening my window, I breathed in the cool evening air. The streets were deserted, which meant no traffic, no skateboarders darting in and out, no pedestrians to consider. It was a school night and young parents would be home with their kids trying to help with homework or hustle the little ones off to bed. Mature adults, which I prefer calling anyone fifty and over, were probably watching TV before turning in. I cut over to Parklawn Avenue and drove to Centennial Park.

Swans drifted across the calm water and I stopped to watch them. That area had always played such a large part in my family life. It was a vibrant place. I couldn't remember how many concerts I'd heard stretched out on a blanket near the pavilion. On weekends, we'd stroll the farmer's market. There were walking trails, bike trails, paddle boats, and beautiful gardens. Centennial Lake Park had been the scene of so many good memories.

I leaned back on the padded headrest and closed my eyes. Slowly I reviewed the crime scene, the cast of characters involved, searching for clues I might have missed.

I must have been there for an hour, and the only thing I'd accomplished was rehashing everything I'd learned so far. Turning the key, I started the jeep. Maybe if I went out to the Pierce mansion again. Maybe if I stopped over thinking it . . .

Yellow crime tape was still draped across the door, but pieces of it had been ripped and flapped in the breeze. Floodlights in front of the stately building were the only illumination, making the place look like a haunted house. I didn't know what I expected to find, but since I was there, I got out of the jeep.

I'd always entered and exited through the front of the building, so I pushed myself in a different direction. Instead of walking straight ahead, I turned to the left and followed a worn path around back where I could see a small guesthouse. A faint light, possibly from a candle, flitted across the walls inside. I walked toward it. Thankfully I'd worn my boots or I might have fallen. The ground was uneven; small holes pitted the lawn. It appeared the gardener hadn't started working in that area yet.

I'd left my bag in the jeep, but even if I had it

with me, a flashlight wasn't inside. I'd have to pick one up next time I went shopping. A ladder stood propped up against the side of the little house, and thankfully the moon was almost full or I wouldn't have been able to see a thing. I kept my head down and crept forward.

My heart raced as I got closer. I started inventing a story to explain being there. Someone was moving around in the guesthouse, I was sure of it. But who could it be? Randolph was the only person allowed on the property, and he was in jail. I mentally went through a checklist of possibilities.

"Git her!"

A man suddenly lunged out of the darkness. Grabbing me from behind, he squeezed tight, pinning me to his chest. I struggled and kicked. "Let me go!"

But that only made him squeeze tighter until I thought I'd pass out.

Another man, the one who had shouted, came running up behind us. "Good," he said to his partner. Then to me he said, "Ya ain't got no business being here—this is private property. If I catch ya again, I'll have ta hurt ya. Understand?"

I should have just nodded, but I didn't. "I'm an officer of the court. When the police find out—"

"This broad's real stupid," the one holding me told his pal.

"Yeah, she don't listen too good."

"Maybe we could leave a little reminder, know what I mean?" He shook me. "So she never goes where she ain't wanted. How about a nice long scar right across yer cheek?" he snarled in my ear.

"I have a gun pointed right at your chest!" a third man shouted. "So you better do what I say and let her go." I recognized that voice.

"Do what the man says," the boss told his flunky. "This ain't worth gettin' killed over."

I was released, so suddenly I fell forward, trying to catch my breath.

"Come over here by me, Kathy," Nathan said.

I ran toward him, ignoring the other two.

I was almost there when a large figure came up behind Nathan and hit him on the head with what looked like a blackjack. As he fell, I tried catching him but wasn't fast enough. Two of the men wore ski masks. They ran toward the third, and I was so concerned with Nathan that I didn't have time to watch which direction they ran.

"Oh my God, Nathan, what in the world were you thinking? How did you get here? Are you okay?"

He was sprawled across the lawn, facedown. I reached out and stroked his head to check for bleeding.

"Ouch!" he groaned.

"At least you're conscious. That's a good sign." He rolled over onto his back and I sat next to him to cradle his head. "What are you doing here?"

"Lizzie was worried. I traced you to the park and followed you here. There's no way in hell I'm losing another Sullivan." He started to sit up but fell back.

"You better lay still a minute."

"I'm fine. But it sure is nice having a woman fuss over me again."

After twenty minutes or so, Nathan felt better and we slowly walked back to our cars. But I couldn't shake the feeling of being watched. Glancing over my shoulder, I was sure there was someone inside the guesthouse. Staring . . .

Chapter Sixteen

I couldn't let Nathan go home with that lump on his head. He had to be checked throughout the night to make sure there was no concussion. So I made him call one of his crew to come pick up his car and took him home with me. He grumbled, saying he'd been hit harder before and came through okay. He'd be fine at home, he insisted.

I ignored him.

As I settled him in with a fresh cup of coffee and a stack of magazines to keep him awake, I said, "I'll be back in two hours, and two hours after that. If there's any sign that you're losing consciousness, I'm hauling you down to emergency."

He didn't have any more arguments left and just sat in the chair he'd collapsed into, nodding.

"And, again, thank you for coming to my rescue." I leaned down and hugged him. "You're my hero."

He touched his head and winced. "Someone has to save you from yourself. But when I feel better I'm going to read you the riot act for going out there alone. Why do you think I introduced you to the gang?"

He didn't give me a chance to answer.

"To help you, that's why. To make sure you don't get hurt. So will you let us do our job?"

"We'll talk about it in the morning." I turned off the lamp. "Good night."

I hadn't planned on telling Lizzie what happened at the mansion, but when she woke up the next morning and found Nathan asleep on the couch, I had to start talking. I've never believed in the concept of lying by omission. If you don't say something, you're not lying. Silence is just a whole lot of nothing. Besides, everyone's not entitled to know every tiny detail about another person's life. And what would be the point in telling her I'd been in danger? I was fine. And then I told a little white lie. It was an age-old ploy parents used to keep their children safe from worry.

I told her about going out to the park—which was true. I even told her about the swans. Nice touch. Then I told her Nathan and I had just happened to run into each other. I was on a roll, so I explained that he often went to the park to clear his head. I think I remember he told me he'd done that once, so that was true, also.

"We chatted awhile," I told her. "And when he was getting back into his car, he hit his head on the frame. Smack. I thought he knocked himself out and ran around to help him. And I couldn't leave him like that, could I? I made him come

129

back here with me so I could take care of him."

I could tell Lizzie liked the part about me taking care of Nathan. She'd always been fond of him. Whether she bought my story or not, she didn't have time to say. When I was finished, the kids were rushing around and Lizzie's phone started ringing. In less than ten minutes, all three of them were out the door.

Nathan took a shower while I made ham and cheese omelets and fried up some potatoes. I was pouring coffee at the table when he walked into the kitchen.

He sat across from me. "This looks great. You shouldn't have gone to so much trouble." His hair was damp and he smelled of coconut soap.

"Is there anything else I can get you?"

"I'm fine, thanks."

As he salted his eggs, I looked for a sign of the lump on his head. "How do you feel?"

"Just a little headache. I found some aspirin in the bathroom and took a few, if that's okay?"

"Take whatever you need."

The food was good, the coffee nice and hot. We were comfortable enough with each other to not feel compelled to fill in the silence. And I was beginning to think he'd forgotten all about the threat he'd made last night. I should have known better.

"Lecture time," he announced after we'd eaten

half our breakfast. "This is a murder case here. Not some run-of-the-mill burglary. One person is dead and there may be more before it's all over. Whoever came after us last night is still out there. I can't guess what their connection to the case is, but until we know what's going on, you can't take chances like you did last night. No more going off by yourself. Got it?"

I smiled.

"I'm not kidding, Kathy." He waited for a reaction.

"I know. And I'll try to—"

He slammed his fork on the table. "There's no trying. You have to be more careful; that's just the way it is."

"You've known me a long time, Nathan. During my career, I made hundreds of arrests. I even apprehended a few murderers. And I've never been hurt or taken chances with the lives of my men."

He didn't have to say it but I knew we were both thinking about Sully. Thankfully, he never brought it up.

"If you're done patting yourself on the back," he said, "I'd like to remind you there's always a first time. You could have been killed last night."

I pushed my plate across the table and picked up the coffee mug. "You're right. As much as I hate to admit it, it was stupid of me to go out there alone. I don't even know what I was looking for. I couldn't sleep last night, afraid those men might have followed us back here. What if I put my family in danger? I guess I just have to face the fact that my time has passed and it's Bostwick's turn now."

I must have sounded pitiful because Nathan's stern expression softened into one of concern.

"Come on, now. We both know Bostwick goes by the book; he doesn't have your instincts or confidence. You have an innate talent, Kathy, and that never goes away. If your gut told you to go rushing out to Buckhorn, there was probably something there. All I'm saying is next time you feel the urge to chase after the bad guys, call me. Okay?"

"I can do that."

"And in case you hadn't noticed," he added, "we're both moving a little slower these days. That's why I hired those kids—for the rough stuff." He laughed. "Think I'm gonna mess up this pretty face? Heck no."

His laugh cheered me up. "It would be a shame. How about a refill?"

"Sure." He held up his mug.

I walked to the counter. "Did you recognize any of those men last night?" I asked.

"No. They had their backs to me. But the big one with the blackjack, his voice sounded familiar."

"That's what I thought." As I poured coffee, I asked, "Did you see someone in the guest-house?"

"It was dark and I wasn't there long enough to get a good look at anything."

"Maybe I imagined it. That old place has got to have a few ghosts floating around."

Nathan nodded in agreement.

"You know, Leland was only one when he died in the mansion," I said. "If I remember right, he had just started walking and fell into the pool. The coroner said it was accidental that the poor baby drowned. But the old man blamed Jackie because she was babysitting him at the time. Guess he was looking for one more reason to hate her."

"Old Marshall T. died at Buckhorn, too, don't forget. If there's a ghost out there, it surely has to be him."

"He was a ghoul," I said. "Everyone in town hated him."

"I never told you this but I've always felt a little guilty about the way we handled things," Nathan said. "Because we all wanted him gone, maybe we weren't thorough enough. We just| took the coroner's word for everything, filled out and filed our reports. We didn't even go out to have a look around."

"Are you kidding?" I asked, sitting back down in my chair. "He was eighty-four years old!

He'd enjoyed bad health for years. You remember how he loved complaining to anyone who'd listen? He had a full-time nurse who attended to him around the clock. His private physician came in to check on him every week. There was a full staff in and around the estate."

Nathan nodded. "I know . . . I know."

"No one lives forever, Nathan."

Chapter Seventeen

Nathan had work to do and called Brock to come pick him up. As I watched them drive away, I realized how tired I was. Locking the door behind me, all I could think about was sleep.

I looked at the clock radio when my phone rang. It was 2:35. I'd been asleep for five hours.

"Mother, I hate to ask but I just remembered I promised Chloe we'd go to the mall after school. Cam will take the bus home but I don't want him to be alone in the house. Can you help him with an art project he's working on? We'll bring home a pizza for dinner."

"No problem. You know I love spending time with Cam."

"Are you okay? You sound funny."

I'd learned a long time ago that people react negatively to the idea of a nap. Adults think it's something only babies and old folks do. Children run screaming when told it's nap time and think they're being punished. Lizzie would have thought I was sick if I admitted to sleeping in the middle of the day. So I just said, "I'm fine. Have fun at the mall."

"We will. Gotta go. Bye."

I had an hour and used it to take a shower and

change into a floral maxi dress. My new haircut was still fighting me—just a week more and things would settle down across my forehead. I was rubbing lotion into my hands when I heard the front door open.

"Grammy!"

"Is that you, Chloe?" I shouted. "Where's your brother?"

"It's me, Cameron." Part of Cam's condition made it difficult for him to catch inflections and nuances in speech. Sarcasm was almost impossible for him to understand.

I hurried to help him with his jacket and backpack. "I knew it was you, sweetie. I was just joking."

He looked confused. "I thought a joke was like knock, knock, who's there?"

"Then I guess I was teasing you."

"Oh."

"Your mom took Chloe to the mall. She told me you're working on a project. How about we do some art together? I brought my paint box and haven't even opened it up the whole time I've been here."

"Cool. I'll go get my stuff."

"Is it something you can do out on the deck? I've been inside all day and need a good dose of fresh air."

"Sure. I'll be right back." He grabbed his things and hurried to his room.

Lizzie kept one of my old easels and a few small canvases in the guest closet. I carried them out to the deck. After setting things up, I wiped off the round, wooden table and went to get my paints and brushes.

Cam beat me back and was pulling one of the deck chairs closer to the table when I got there. A box of old wooden blocks was in front of him, and he began lightly touching the surface of each one.

After we were both situated, I asked, "So what are you going to do with those blocks?"

"We're supposed to make a mosaic, only not with tiles. We're supposed to make a design out of things we have at home. Some kids are using pieces of cardboard. Wendy Stark's using her brother's old baseball cards."

"Let's hope he doesn't want them anymore."

Cam giggled. "I know."

The view from Lizzie's deck was beautiful. Early spring green streaked the lawn; trees were still hungover from winter but tiny buds stood ready to unfold along their branches. Pink and yellow crocuses poked through the grass to get some sun. Dozens of red and orange tulips lined the white fence along the property line. Off in the distance, on the other side of a mossy hill, an aquamarine lake sparkled. Birds chirped as they circled the water.

I checked to see if I'd brought just the right

colors I'd need. But out of the corner of my eye, I watched Cam working. His concentration reminded me of other moments we'd shared. Before he could talk, we finger-painted. After a trip to the zoo one time, we made little animals out of molding clay. And there was the time we sat for hours cutting snowflakes from red and green construction paper to decorate the house at Christmas. There were so many projects I couldn't remember them all. But I always remembered our conversations.

"Have you seen pictures of the tiled mosaics in Mexico? Hundreds of little pieces of ceramic, all put together making one beautiful picture. Some of them have lasted for hundreds of years. When I was in Mexico City I saw a really big one at the university there."

"Our teacher, Mrs. Tucker, showed us a movie. But we're not supposed to make pictures like they did. Ours are supposed to be modern. Just shapes and colors. I think this is better. Then we don't have to try to make it look perfect. Know what I mean, Grammy?"

"I know exactly what you mean, sweetie."

I thought about the landscape I was painting and wondered if it was time to try a different style. "Do you think you'll finish your project while I'm here? I want to see how it turns out."

"I'm almost done already." He held up a block. "See? I painted some of them. They had to dry a few days but they're okay now, so I could move them around." He started taking all the blocks out of the box and put them on the table. "What are you working on, Grammy?"

"A landscape. The view from here is so pretty, and this way I can always remember it. You've seen some of my paintings, haven't you?"

"Sure. Mom has one in her bedroom. She says it's the house she grew up in when she was a little girl. It's nice. Can you paint a picture of this house so I can always remember it, too?"

"Why didn't I think of that?"

Cleaning my brush, I watched as he turned the blocks over and over, trying to decide which pattern pleased him the most. Some were faded and hadn't gotten a coat of paint. Some were chipped; some were smooth and shiny. The more he worked, the more intrigued I became.

"When your mom and Chloe finish at the mall, they're picking up a pizza for dinner."

"Better not have peppers on it. I hate peppers."

"If it does, I'll pick them off for you."

"Thanks, Grammy."

When the light had changed and the air cooled, I asked Cameron, "Are you almost done?"

"Almost. I just have to glue these blocks in the frame."

"You can do that while I put my things away."

"Cool."

• • •

After the pizza was gone and the house was quiet, I called Nathan to see how he was feeling.

"An ice pack does wonders," he said, sounding upbeat. "How about you?"

"I just watched the news and there doesn't seem to be anything . . . new."

"Well I have something to report. Polly found out who made the nine-one-one call that night. That girl's amazing. There isn't a system out there she can't hack into."

"You mean she hacked into the phones at the police station?"

"I told you she was good."

"I'm impressed. So who was it?"

"A guy named Mike DeGroot. He and his girl found the body."

"So why wasn't he there when the police arrived?"

Nathan sighed. "He's just some dumb jock. He and his buddies—every one of them underage—went out there to drink, thinking the place was deserted. You know how kids are. I tell you, each new crop seem to think they're entitled to do whatever they please."

Sometimes Nathan got sidetracked and needed a slight nudge. "So they were out there drinking and . . . ?"

"Well, Mike's got his girl with him, and they go upstairs for some privacy."

"They must have been scared out of their minds when they found Stacey," I said.

"You called that one right. Mike said his girl started to make the call right away but he grabbed her phone away from her. That's when they took off for downstairs and got the hell out of there. But a few miles down the road, they pulled over. The girl's hysterical by now, begging him to call the cops. So he drives to a gas station where he used to work, 'cause they got a pay phone. And he calls from there, thinking the number can't be traced."

"But Polly did trace it. This is great. Let's go out there and—"

"Hold your horses. I already did." I could hear the pride in his voice.

"When?"

"About two hours ago. I talked to the owner. Can you believe it? He's a third cousin or something like that to DeGroot. I'll never understand why the kid didn't go somewhere no one knew him."

"But why was he being so secretive if he hadn't done anything wrong?" I asked.

"Mike DeGroot doesn't exactly have a stellar record. DUIs, car theft, and one count of breaking and entering. He hates cops and figured they'd finger him for the murder. Said he knows how things 'go down.' Says he watches true crime shows and the cops always suspect the spouse first and the innocent neighbor who reports the crime second."

"Not all the time," I said. "But it's usually the best place to start looking. So you talked to him?" I asked.

"First I had to listen to his cousin for twenty minutes telling me how Mike may be a screw-up but he'd never kill anyone. But he finally made the call and convinced the kid to come talk to me. I waited half an hour before he showed up."

"You interviewed him right there?" I asked. "In the gas station?"

"Sure did. At first he was difficult, but he finally broke down when I threatened to take him in. He told me the same story as his cousin. That he'd never kill anyone and didn't even know Stacey Jordan."

"And you believed him?"

"Well, you've always said I'm an excellent judge of character," Nathan chided.

"Yes, I have."

"I believed DeGroot before we strapped him up to the polygraph and even more afterwards."

"What polygraph?"

"After we talked awhile, I persuaded him to come with me back to the office."

"Well you certainly have been a busy boy," I said. "So there's one less suspect on the list."

"On our list—he's still on Bostwick's. And you know why?"

I was getting ready to say I didn't know why, but Nathan was too quick for me.

"I'll tell you why. Because he's going by the book. Didn't I tell you? He's working on subpoenaing phone records. All that red tape will keep him tied up for at least a week."

"And what about the surveillance system at the mansion? Couldn't Polly just look at it?"

"It was disconnected that night. Has been since Randolph started the renovations. He just wanted people to think it was hooked up; he planned to install a fancy new one when the work was done."

"Wow." I couldn't believe his carelessness. "Guess the big city man still has a small town mentality."

"You'd think Mr. Big Shot would know that the days of leaving your front door unlocked are long gone," Nathan said.

Sadly, I agreed.

Chapter Eighteen

So what had I accomplished so far? As I stared out the kitchen window, trying to wake up, I thought about the past couple of days.

Antoine Rousseau, a man who knew Stacey Jordan in only a professional capacity, had an airtight alibi for the night she was killed. The man who initially found her body had passed a polygraph test. I agreed with Nathan that Mike DeGroot and his girlfriend had just been at the wrong place at the wrong time. Besides, the guy had no connection to Stacey at all, which almost always meant that he had no reason to murder her. The list of workers who'd been going in and out of the mansion for weeks was long. Could Stacey have been having an affair with one of them? Lust has always been one of the most common motives for murder. Guess it was time to start going down the list of carpenters, painters, and gardeners Lizzie had given me. But would I be wasting my time?

Randolph Pierce still headed my list of suspects. He'd known Stacey and was seen fighting with her by several people. That day in the gallery, I'd gotten the feeling he hated her. What could she have possibly done to get him so angry? She'd told me that she could write a book about the Pierce family secrets. Was she blackmailing Randolph?

"TGIF!" Chloe startled me as she blew into the room. Her tattoo had washed off, finally, and she stood in front of me all smiles. Spinning around, she held her arms open. "How do you like my new outfit, Grandma? This is the exact same blouse that was on the cover of last month's *Seventeen*. Isn't it hashtag amazing?"

Her blouse was a white eyelet tunic with red ribbons woven through the long sleeves. She looked like a flower child from the sixties. In fact, I think I'd worn something very similar when I was her age. I smiled remembering how very cool I felt back then. Love beads around my neck, my hair in a perfect flip. That was all it took when I was thirteen to make my world groovy.

"Totally amazing. You look so pretty, Chloe."

For the moment, she was happy with herself—and me. After a few more spins, she gave me a quick kiss. "See ya later, Grandma." And she ran off to get her jacket.

Cameron came next. Slowly walking into the room, he held his art project in front of him like it was made of glass instead of wood and metal. Then, ever so carefully, he laid it down on the table in front of me.

"What do you think?" he asked. His expression

was so serious; I knew my opinion meant a lot to him.

"From what I can see, it's great, Cam. Is the glue dry so I can pick it up and get a closer look?"

"Sure. You can study it while I get dressed." As he walked away from me, I watched his focus go from the blocks to his feet. Each step was so measured, his head down, causing him to almost bump into his mother as he left the room.

"We'll be out of your hair soon," Lizzie said, adjusting her earring. "How are things coming with the murder investigation? Randolph's going out of his mind in jail. Do you have any good news I can pass on? Anything?"

I thought a moment. Letting him know that another suspect had been proven innocent wouldn't exactly make him jump for joy. "Tell him that I'm working with a crew of experts and we'll let him know the minute we come up with something." I smiled and drank my coffee.

"Guess that's all he can ask. Oh, by the way, there's a walkathon tomorrow, if you want to come walk . . . or watch. It's a fund raiser for autistic research. I'm on the committee; my office is one of the sponsors. Should be a beautiful day for it."

"I like walking; it's one of my favorite modes of transportation," I joked. "Can I let you know later?"

146

"Sure," she said. "And don't worry about the kids or dinner tonight. I usually work a half day on Fridays and we eat leftovers or sandwiches when we get home. No lessons for the kids, no running around for me. Nice and simple."

"I might go see Nathan; I'll let you know."

Lizzie came closer to make eye contact. "I'm really glad you're here, Mother. Have I told you that enough? And thanks for helping with this case. Sometimes I feel so overwhelmed with the kids and work. There's always so much to do I feel like I can't . . ."

"Hey," I stood up and smoothed down her collar, "stop looking at the big picture—it's way too scary. And listen to your mother when she tells you that everything you're afraid will happen very rarely does. And things you wish for come even more rarely. It's the unexpected you can always count on to mess with you. And you can't prepare for the unknown, so what's the point of worrying?"

Lizzie hugged me. "I don't know what I'd do without you."

Right in the middle of our mother-daughter moment, Lizzie's cell phone went off. "Sorry," she said, "I gotta get that."

"I know."

Alone again, I sat back down to study Cam's art.

Five blocks had been arranged horizontally

and six diagonally. They'd all been glued into an ebony frame. The effect was interesting, and I picked up the piece to touch each square.

Right in the middle was a block that had been painted a glossy silver and then brushed over lightly with black. Next to it was an alphabet block that looked brand new. The letter C embossed in the center was painted dark blue. A pink one, scuffed and old, was next to it, making their juxtaposition seem familiar to me in some strange way. There was a chipped block painted red next to one with a duck sticker on top of gold. As I held the piece and turned it, I felt as though I could almost see into Cam's creative soul. All the shapes and colors represented emotions he was unable to express in a conventional way. The end result was glorious and unique, just like he was.

I put the frame down and got up to scrounge for some breakfast. Cam ran back into the kitchen.

"Mom says she'll call you; she's out in the car with Chloe." He picked up his project, turning it to what he intended to be right side up.

"Your art is awesome, Cam. I love it. No doubt you'll get an A."

"Will you be here when I get home?" he asked. "'Cause Lewis's mom said she'd take us to a movie—if she has time. But I'll see you after that. Okay?"

"I'm sticking around; we've got plenty of time. Not to worry." I hugged him.

He smiled and started toward the door. Then, unexpectedly, he turned around and held the frame up over his head. "Maybe later we can hang this on the wall, next to your painting, Grammy."

"Our own little art gallery. That would be perfect."

As Cam stood there, in that light, at that distance, I suddenly saw the blocks differently. Now I knew why they had seemed familiar and yet unsettling. They had all reminded me of Jacqueline Bannister-Pierce.

The silver triggered the memory of her tattered old gown. Her wrinkled face was represented by the scuffed block. Pink was the silly little girl color she'd worn the last time I'd seen her. The blocks—a child's toy, painted and set in a frame trying to appear sophisticated—were just like Jackie. The old and new blocks next to each other were like Jackie and her boy toy, side by side. And the blocks themselves were pieces in a mosaic like the stones in her bracelet—a modern bracelet hanging on her sagging wrist. I must have filed the image away in my subconscious. Now as I thought about it, that sleek jeweled cuff seemed out of place.

Chapter Nineteen

I spent the morning checking out Randolph's alibi. A cashier at Red's told me on the phone she remembered Randolph picking up a pizza because he had become a regular customer. She had also seen his face on the news when he was taken in. I went on the computer and looked up the episodes of *Mad Men* that had aired that night and decided to see if Randolph's memory of the plot lines matched up. Then I left the house to go and see Randolph at the jail.

It was drizzling a nice warm rain. After backing the jeep out of the garage, I pulled the hood of my jacket up over my head. I'd rather get a little damp than bother with an umbrella. Dry or wet, they just get in the way.

Traffic was heavy and moved slowly. Fridays were always like that. The trip to the jail was taking much longer than usual. As I sat in line to get through yet another stop light, I thought about the case.

The one thing criminals had in common, I'd learned my first year on the force, was the belief they had been blessed with superior intelligence. They were always so sure they could outsmart the cops. Seeing their expression slowly go from smug to frightened as they realized we'd figured out their game was one of my guilty pleasures. The Pierce family had always thought they were smarter than the entire population of Edina. There could be dozens of motives for Randolph to have killed Stacey. It could be greed—Stacey could have been stealing from him. It could be sex— they could have been having an affair. But for Lizzie's sake, I decided to stop my train of thought.

The officer at the front desk was an unfamiliar face, but I knew the guard who escorted me back to Randolph's cell. He was Stanley Nelson's son, Max.

"I ran into your dad at the airport when I got to town. He looks good."

Max nodded. "He was driving us crazy, especially Mom. Being home all the time, he just didn't know what to do with himself." He laughed. "When he started rearranging everything in the kitchen, it was either get a part-time job or his own apartment."

"Well he seems happy. And you . . . I remember when you were in grade school. How long have you been a court officer?"

"Almost a year now."

"You like it? Because it's true what they say about life being too long to suffer every day at a job you hate."

"I hear that," Max said. "But I'm one of the lucky ones. I love what I do."

"Good." I patted his shoulder.

"Mr. Pierce is with his lawyer now, but since that's your daughter and you're the investigator on the case, I don't think there's a problem." He winked. "It was nice seeing you, Mrs. Sullivan. Take care."

They didn't move right away. Maybe they thought it was just the guard coming to check up on Randolph. Whatever the reason, I was able to observe Lizzie and Randolph for a candid moment while they held hands and smiled lovingly at each other.

And I didn't like it . . . one bit.

Of course I'd heard the words when she told me they had feelings for each other. I'd listened when Randolph said he loved my daughter. But that was far different than actually seeing them there right in front of me. Very different. The reality of their emotions was unsettling.

"Lizzie," I said.

She jumped away from him like he was on fire. "Mother! What are you doing here?"

Randolph sat silently, looking down at his cuffed hands.

"That's an odd question. I'm working to get Randolph out of jail. Isn't that what you're doing here?"

Lizzie took a handful of papers out of her briefcase. "Of course."

"Grab a chair, Mrs. Sullivan," Randolph said,

pointing to the corner. "I'm glad you came. Lizzie and I were just discussing calling you. There's something you need to know."

I dragged a chair to Lizzie's side of the table, which separated us from Randolph. I couldn't let either of them see how anxious I was. Well, angry would describe my feelings more accurately. But I couldn't figure out if I was angry that my daughter had feelings for a man whose family I'd barely tolerated for years or if I was angry that of all the men in world, she'd fallen in love with one who might be a murderer. So I sat down and waited until one of them spoke.

Lizzie glared at Randolph, signaling him to stay quiet. "You go first, Mother. Why are you here? You never mentioned anything this morning about coming to the jail."

Okay, if that's the way she wanted to play it, I'd go along. "I just wanted to verify a few things with Randolph regarding his alibi."

"Oh, uh, maybe we should go first, then," Lizzie said.

"Let me tell her." Randolph patted Lizzie's hand.

Lizzie's eyes flitted from me to Randolph while she blinked back a tear. All the while his face remained stoic.

"The reason I haven't taken a polygraph is because . . . because I . . ."

"Randy was with me the night Stacey was

killed," Lizzie blurted out. "I've begged him to take the test, but he doesn't want to involve me. He thinks he's protecting me and the kids. But I'm his alibi. If I have to, I'll come forward and recuse myself."

Randolph smiled at Lizzie. "I'd never do anything to hurt your daughter, Mrs. Sullivan. You have to believe me." He looked across the table at me, waiting for some reassuring words to come flowing out of my mouth so he could feel better about himself.

But I didn't have any to give.

"Why should I believe another word when you swore you were alone that night? You told me how you got a pizza, watched TV—even named a specific program. I've just wasted my morning."

"And you." I looked at Lizzie. "That whole story about an abused woman needing your help? Were you even at the office that night or did you lie to me, too?"

"Please, Mother, don't be mad. I was at the office when Randy called about a legal matter—I swear it's the truth. After I handled things there, I drove out to his place."

"What kind of legal matter?" I asked. "And be forewarned that I'm only going to believe half of what you tell me."

"You've heard the stories for years, Mother. We all have. About priceless art hidden in the walls of the mansion. Randy's done a lot of research—here and in Europe. He's positive the stories are true and needed advice—legal advice about where he stands when the painting is eventually found."

"That's the truth, Mrs. Sullivan. Grandfather went on and on about the Klimt, how he had it smuggled out of Europe and went to great lengths to hide it. He'd cackle, telling us how the rest of the world thought the painting had been destroyed by Nazis in a fire, but only he knew the real truth. Dad always laughed it off. Everyone did. The old man was more than eccentric. But every lie has a grain of truth. Isn't that what they say?"

"Yes."

"So what if it's true? What if his outrageous story is true? Art lovers like us would flock to see the painting. The papers would be full of the story. And all the questions would start flying. Where did it come from? How did it end up at Buckhorn? Who brought it there? And the world would know my grandfather was a thief. Next would come lawyers knocking on my door, all of them eager to sue the estate and the last remaining relatives. Everyone with their hand out, wanting compensation. I don't have much, Mrs. Sullivan. It would not only ruin me financially but my good name. I have to protect myself."

"You're right," I grudgingly agreed. "But you're not in here because of stolen art; you're in here on a murder charge. I understand now why you wouldn't take a lie detector test but what about the DNA?" I asked. "Why wouldn't you let them take a sample?"

"Lizzie told you that I fought with Stacey and how she ended up scratching my face. It was just an accident, nothing serious. In fact, by the time the police arrested me and took photos of my body, there really wasn't much to see. But we all know that it only takes a little DNA to convict someone. There must have been some of mine under her nails."

"When was your fight?" I asked.

"The morning she was killed."

"While she was alive, right?" I asked.

He nodded. "Right."

"And you don't think she would have washed her hands throughout the day, maybe several times?"

"Sure."

"So why wouldn't your DNA have been washed away by the time her body was found?"

"There still could have been a microscopic amount left. That's all it takes."

"I'll get a copy of the report and we'll deal with whatever it says. But everything's changed now," I told them both. "Randolph, you're going to take that test and let them swab your mouth for DNA. Lizzie, you're going to vouch for him. You're both going to cooperate fully with the police." She started to protest but I wouldn't let her. "The main thing is getting Randolph out of here, right?

You've done nothing wrong. Maybe you'll have to step back and let another attorney handle this, but you can assist."

We all took a few seconds to breathe.

"So now you know everything," Lizzie finally said.

"Do I?"

Randolph looked upset. "I'm so sorry, Mrs. Sullivan. I know it won't do any good, but I promise you, from now on out, no secrets."

Lizzie held back tears. "Me, too. Please, Mother, we need your help here. Randy's innocent."

"You hired me to do a job," I finally told her, "and I'm going to do it. My feelings are hurt but that's not important to this investigation." I started to stand up then remembered a question I'd been meaning to ask Randolph Pierce.

"Who were you talking to that day I was in the gallery? You sounded so angry."

"It was me," Lizzie said. "We'd both had a bad day . . . it was a silly argument. Nothing to it. Really."

"Well, it didn't sound like nothing from my end."

Randolph looked embarrassed. "I commented on how nice Stacey looked that day and Lizzie overreacted."

"No, what you said was Stacey had great legs." Then Lizzie looked at me and said, "See, I told you it was stupid."

I just smiled.

Chapter Twenty

I rushed out of the jail needing to hear a friendly voice and see an honest face. So I called Nathan.

"Can you meet me at the diner for lunch? I really need to talk."

"Are you okay, Kathy?" His concern almost made me go weepy but I fought the urge.

"I'm at the jail. I had a few things to run by Randolph. Imagine my surprise when I walked in and found him holding hands with my daughter."

"Lizzie and Pierce? Are you sure?"

"Lizzie told me days ago that she's always had feelings for him. And later he told me he felt the same. But I guess I thought she was just feeling sorry for him. Maybe I'd hoped it would just all go away."

"You weren't ready to hear them. And now they're up in your face and you can't look away," he said. "That had to be tough. But why were you there in the first place?"

I sat in the jeep, still parked in front of the jail, and unloaded all the facts and my frustrations on my best friend. I told Nathan my suspicions about Jackie, about Randolph's real alibi and my daughter's involvement in a murder investigation.

When I was finished, he said, "You'll have to give me a minute to digest all this."

"Imagine how I feel! Both of them lying to me like that. I feel so stupid."

"Hold up! You have nothing to feel stupid about, Kathy. You're out there just trying to help them and they lie to you. What are you supposed to do with that?"

"I don't know."

"Look, I just had a meeting with my crew. I think you'll be happy with the progress they've made. Why don't the six of us all meet around one? We can talk more about Lizzie and—"

"No! This part is personal. I don't want your people to know anything about it. What my daughter and her client do is none of their business. It has nothing to do with our case."

After a moment, he agreed. "You're right. It's none of their business."

"Thanks, Nathan. I knew I could count on you."

"Always, Kathy."

I got to the Twelfth before any of the others arrived. The diner was crowded and noisy. The same tall man who had been there last time greeted me.

"Will there be just one for lunch today?" he asked.

"No, there'll be six of us. And would it be

159

possible to have that large booth in the corner?" I pointed.

"Sure. But you'll have to give us about ten minutes to clear it off."

"That's fine."

According to my watch, it was 12:35. I had just enough time for a quick trip to the ladies room to make sure I didn't look as frazzled as I felt. When I came out, the booth was ready; menus and silverware had been arranged at three places on each side of the table.

I scooted across the long bench seat so I could be next to the window and ordered an iced tea—no lemon.

The waitress nodded, knowingly. "You saw *60 Minutes*, too, huh?"

We exchanged a look as if we belonged to a secret club. And then she left to get my drink.

There had been so many reports lately about bar fruit being contaminated. According to the last health update, orange slices, lemon wedges, and cherries were almost lethal. I never paid much attention, though, because next week the experts would change their collective minds and urge everyone to slice citrus fruits and leave them out in the open for at least a day. They'd swear that if all good citizens complied, they'd never get diabetes or maybe add five years to their lives. But it didn't matter what any expert said; I'd just never liked lemons.

A loud roar made me look out the window. Rosie sat on a motorcycle, taking off her helmet. I watched as she ran a few fingers through her hair and got off the bike. Then she snapped to attention and walked toward the diner.

When she came through the door, I waved so she'd see me in the corner.

"Hey, Katie," she said. "How's it hangin'?"

I looked down at myself. "So far, so good. How about yourself?"

"Can't complain." Then she flagged the waitress down and ordered a diet Coke.

"We're the first ones here," I told her.

"So we are." She seemed uncomfortable with me, and I hoped that maybe by the end of lunch, we'd get past that.

Then I saw Polly enter the diner.

"Hey, Pol!" Rosie shouted across the room.

Polly turned heads as she hurried toward our corner. A tight, leather micro-miniskirt showed off her great legs, which were covered to the knees by black leather boots. She had a cropped T-shirt, and when she moved, her bare midriff peeked through. On top of that was a faded jean jacket.

"Hey." She sat next to Rosie—across from me. "The guys are going to be late. Nathan said we should go ahead and eat; they'll be here in about an hour," she told me. Then, to Rosie, she said, "In the meantime we can fill Katherine in on what we've been doing."

"Good deal," Rosie said. "But let's order first; I'm starving big time."

The three of us talked about food while looking over the menu. It really seemed to be the perfect icebreaker as we compared likes and dislikes, all-time favorite meals, and restaurants.

When the waitress finally came, Polly ordered a small salad because she was on a diet and water with three lemon wedges. The waitress raised her eyebrows and glanced over at me as if to say, "She doesn't know what we do." Rosie decided on the meatloaf, and I ordered the same.

After the menus had been collected and the three of us were left alone, I said, "I'm glad things worked out this way. Gives us a chance to know each other better."

Polly smiled. "I'm glad, too."

"Likewise," Rosie agreed.

There was an uncomfortable pause before Polly kicked things off. "So I've been checking Henry Slater out. There's a lot out there about this guy. None of it good."

I thought about the last time I'd seen Hank. It had been outside Pierce Gallery. Or maybe it had been that night at the guesthouse. I still had my suspicions that he'd been the one who clubbed Nathan.

"I've only met him a few times; all I really know is he used to play football, lives in Vegas, and sponges off older, rich women," I told them.

Polly nodded and grinned. "He was third string for the Rams and only played in one game. Can you believe it?"

Rosie laughed. "A real one-hit wonder."

"Oh, he could have had a successful career but he screwed it all up when he went out with his buddies on a Fourth of July weekend. One of the guys had a boat and they took it out on Lake Havasu—"

"That's in Arizona, ain't it?" Rosie asked.

"Yep." Polly said. "So they're out on the boat, partying. For two days nothing but booze, women, and drugs. Everything was good . . . until the last day. As they were heading home, Slater's so drunk that he falls off and gets his foot caught in the boat's propeller. From the hospital reports I read, he was lucky he survived. But his foot was cut clear down to the bone."

I was waiting for the part that might make me feel sorry for Hank but so far I hadn't heard it.

"Geez," is all Rosie said.

"So there's operations, which means lots of pain killers. He's cut from the team, naturally, and along the way gets addicted to his meds."

"Addiction means money and being desperate for money usually leads to crime," I said.

Polly nodded in agreement. "You should know, Chief."

"And Las Vegas is definitely not the best place for an addict to be," Rosie added. "I've seen way too many people end up dead out there."

"Slater's like a cockroach," Polly continued. "He'll always survive. You should see his arrest records. They go back ten years. Mostly petty stuff—anything to get money for his habits, which now include coke and gambling. He's been banned from two casinos for trying to steal money from several people at the blackjack table. He's been to rehab five times. On the third visit, to a place in Malibu, he met a wealthy socialite. When they got out, he moved in with her at her house on the beach."

"Sounds like a real lowlife," Rosie said, playing with her fork.

"That seemed to be around the time he started targeting older, lonely, rich women."

"How many have there been before Jackie?" I asked.

"I've found an even dozen so far. He only stays with them until he gets the money. Sometimes he's working on more than one poor woman at a time. I found two restraining orders issued by judges in two different cities in Nevada. There's even a complaint filed by the grown children of one of the women, claiming Slater drugged and then coerced their mother into writing a new will, leaving everything to him."

I was stunned. "I just figured Slater was a dumb jock, but now I'm thinking he's a dangerous jock."

"The guy's on steroids, too," Polly said.

"Which makes him the kind of crazy that's scary. He can go from zero to a hundred in no time if something sets him off."

Hank Slater was turning out to be more unstable than I could have ever imagined. "So was Jackie after or before the Malibu lady?"

Polly looked at me through strands of long bangs. "About two months after that poor woman died."

I leaned in a little closer. "And how did she die?"

"There was a bad storm one night—high winds, power outages. The next day neighbors were out, walking the area to assess property damage, and saw her door had been blown off. They found her lying in the middle of the living room. She'd been hit from behind by a piece of wood. The coroner ruled it accidental, probably caused by flying debris. But rumors are floating around the Internet that she was murdered."

"After what you've found, I'm sure it was Slater who hit Nathan on the head out at Buckhorn. A muscle-bound coward who strikes from behind. That seems to be his MO."

"He does love to flex his muscles," Polly said. "In an interview on YouTube, he claimed to have been a bodyguard for several celebrities. But of course he was unable to name any of them because of confidentiality agreements he'd signed."

"Translation: 'I'm lyin',' " Rosie said.

Polly laughed. "Good one, Roe."

"I've also done some checking on Jacqueline

Bannister-Pierce. Now that's one pitiful woman," Polly said.

"Having lived here most of my life, I probably know a lot of what you found out." I went on to fill in some of our local history for the women.

"But did you know that many of her so-called trips to resorts and exclusive spas have actually been to psychiatric hospitals?" Polly asked. "Her last husband had her committed twice."

Okay, she got me there. "No, I never heard about that. But then we weren't supposed to, right?"

"Mrs. Bannister-Pierce has spent hundreds of thousands in hush money."

I couldn't resist asking, "So how much is she worth now?"

"According to bank statements and investment records, her debt outweighs her worth. She's managed to stay afloat on Social Security and by selling off some property she inherited, but now she's out of options. And she's convinced there's some priceless painting at the estate. She's been contacting experts and dealers regarding a particular one by Gustav Klimt."

"Which supposedly was destroyed in a fire during the war," I said.

Polly nodded. "But Mrs. Pierce has been telling everyone that it survived and she can prove it. I found e-mails she sent to an expert at Sotheby's wanting to know the painting's value and checking on the possibility of it going to auction."

"But if the piece was stolen, it would have to be returned to the Austrian government, wouldn't it?" I asked.

"I guess so," Polly said.

"Not if you know the right people," Rosie said. "It can end up in a private collection somewhere and no one's the wiser." She rolled her eyes. "Those fancy auction houses get their computers hacked all the time. There's a whole underground market out there. And when millions are involved, everybody and his brother come out of the woodwork, sniffin' around. My sources tell me some heavyweights are circling the mansion like vultures. Those stories the old lady tells get around. And crazy or not, people are gonna think it's worth a look-see. If what I'm hearing is true, something's going down out there—and soon."

"Could be Jackie's bringing all this danger with her and not even knowing it," I said.

"It's always about greed, isn't it?" Polly asked. "Everybody wanting what they don't have, desperately trying to snatch it away from those who have too much and want something else. It's an endless struggle. If only people could just be happy with what they have," she said wistfully.

I was surprised by how innocent Polly seemed at that moment.

"Well that ain't never gonna happen," Rosie said. "Never."

I had to agree with her.

Chapter Twenty-One

Nathan, E.T., and Brock arrived when the three of us were almost finished eating.

"That looks good," Brock said, craning his neck to locate a waitress.

"Sorry we're late." Nathan looked at me, concerned. "How you doin', Kathy?"

"I'm fine. How are you?" I raised my eyebrows, hoping he'd take the hint to keep my personal problems to himself. "Polly and Rosie have been filling me in. Looks like things are heating up about this stolen painting everyone's so eager to find at the mansion."

E.T. rearranged his silverware while I spoke. Still not satisfied, he picked up his spoon and started rubbing it with a napkin. "I've been out to Buckhorn the last two nights. Security sucks, that's for sure. I had no problem at all getting into that guesthouse. And I can tell you this: someone's definitely living there. Maybe as many as three people, but definitely two. One closet was crammed with all sorts of tacky clothes—women's clothes. Another had men's things. It has to be that Pierce woman and Slater."

"Were you able to figure out who attacked us?" I asked.

"There were three of them that night. I could

make out their footprints. The one who hit Nathan was the largest." E.T. looked over the menu while he spoke. "Do you think they have anything that's not fried in this place? Something vegetarian?" he asked, looking around the restaurant. "No, I guess not."

"This guy's into all that feng shui, Zen, meditation stuff," Nathan told me. "Can you imagine never eating a thick, juicy steak? You don't know what you're missing, man," he told E.T.

"And you, my friend, don't know how good you could feel if you stopped filling your body with preservatives and red meat. More energy, clearer head, you'd feel ten years younger, Boss. Trust me."

"Translation: 'Don't trust another word this guy says,'" Rosie shouted.

We all had to laugh, even E.T.

"Where's that waitress?" Brock asked after we calmed down. "I'm dyin' here."

"You guys order," I told the men. "And I thank you," I smiled at Polly then Rosie. "You've given me a lot to go on." I grabbed a napkin and wiped my mouth. "If you'll excuse me, I think I'll go out to Buckhorn—"

"Not by yourself, you won't," Nathan said, looking panicked. "I've read all the reports and the five of us have had several meetings. Things are heating up out there. No telling who you'll run into."

"You of all people know I can handle myself," I told him.

"You can be as confident as you want, Mrs. Sullivan, but that won't protect you from a bullet," Brock said. "Brave men end up just as dead as cowardly ones."

"Why are you so set on going out there?" Nathan asked. "What do you expect to find that'll clear Randolph?"

"The only thing Bostwick has so far is Randolph's lack of an alibi—well and the fact that he rubs everyone in town the wrong way. What could he possibly have to gain from Stacey's death?" I wondered aloud.

"Oh, it could be a lot of things. Didn't you tell me she mentioned being able to write a book about what she'd seen and heard at the mansion? Maybe she was blackmailing him or threatening him in some way," Nathan said.

"Well, you've given me a lot to think about on the drive over." I stood up.

"Do you even care that I'm hungry and would like to eat something before we go chasing around town?"

"Don't play the guilt card, Nathan. It won't work. If you're hungry, stay and eat. If you insist on coming with me—come."

"You're one bullheaded woman," he said. "Scoot over," he told Brock. "I'll see all of you at the office tomorrow."

After saying good-bye to everyone, I headed for the door with Nathan trailing behind.

Okay, so I did feel a little guilty and stopped at a drive-thru to get Nathan a burger but mostly to quiet down his stomach, which had been growling the entire time. It was a half-hour trip to Buckhorn and I couldn't take the noise any longer. Besides, while he was eating, he'd be unable to scold me anymore.

I switched on the radio. An instrumental version of a Madonna song was playing. Once edgy and controversial, the song had upset parents as well as the Catholic Church. I remembered seeing demonstrations in front of record stores, back in the olden days when there were record stores. But over the years it had made its inevitable journey to easy listening. Born to MTV, it had moved down to VH1, then Muzak. Now it was piped into elevators and waiting rooms. The very same people who had been outraged just a few years previously now listened happily, swaying to the piano and cello arrangement.

People are like that, too, I guess. Their rough edges get smoothed out over time. Jacqueline used to be the talk of the town—literally. Gossiped about, envied, beautiful, and rich. And now, if it wasn't for her strange appearance, she wouldn't be noticed at all. But had all her anger and resentment toward her father evened out over time?

And Henry Slater. Once a professional football player, popular and handsome, he had everything going for him. But drugs and alcohol make men mean; I'd seen it hundreds of times. Slater had hit bottom and was running scared. From what I'd heard, he was all rough edges. About the only thing smoothed out on him was his brain.

As I drove up to the mansion, I could see several vehicles parked out front. A sleek black rental car was on the far side of the driveway. On the other side were two police cars. I sat there a moment, unsure what to do next.

"So what's the plan, Chief?" Nathan still seemed a little miffed with me.

Before I had to admit I didn't really have a plan, Dean Bostwick came walking out the front door. Maybe if I just backed out of the drive-way, I thought foolishly, he wouldn't even know we'd been there. But that was just wishful thinking. As if reading my mind, Bostwick's head snapped around and his eyes focused in on mine.

"Sullivan!" he shouted, motioning me to pull up and park.

"You're in trouble now," Nathan teased. "That man sure doesn't look happy to see you."

"Tell me something I don't know."

Chapter Twenty~Two

"Might as well get this over with," I told Nathan as I parked the jeep in front of Buckhorn.

"Want me to come with you?"

"No thanks, I'm fine. In fact it's probably better if I go alone." I left the engine running and went over to talk to Bostwick.

I missed my police uniform but was glad I'd put on my black pants suit that day. Clothes relay a person's self-image and trigger a subconscious response. Black was a serious color; the matching jacket and pants meant business. The blouse could have ruined the effect if it had been a soft girlie color like pink, so I'd chosen grey. No distracting accessories; only a small pair of silver hoop earrings. Knowing I'd be going to the jail to see Randolph, I had to wear serious clothes to be taken seriously. But even as the day presented some unexpected challenges, I felt confident to handle them.

The sun was shining in his eyes, and Bostwick held a hand up to shield them. "I'm surprised you found your way back out here, so far from the city."

"What do you want, Dean?"

"Word's gotten back to me that you're sticking your nose in my case . . . again. I don't like it when a civilian interferes with official police work."

"I've been hired by Randolph Pierce's attorney as an investigator. But I'm sure you already knew that."

"So now you're an investigator? Like that old guy on TV, what was his name?" Bostwick looked up at the sky, acting like he was trying to remember Barnaby Jones. But I knew he was just getting a kick out of wasting my time.

"Look, I'm investigating the murder of Stacey Jordan, trying to clear my client's name. We both know you don't have enough evidence to go to trial. You just needed a warm body to point a finger at while you figure this whole thing out. Maybe you're a little afraid you're in over your head here, but that's not for me to say. Anyway, get used to me being around because I'm not leaving until the real killer is caught. Now we can play nice and maybe share some information, or we can keep sparring and work against each other."

"You can't be serious!" he shouted. "You expect me to work with you? I did that for way too many years when I was just a lowly cop and you were the grand dame. But that was then and this is how it is today. You're retired. In with the new, which means *me,* Mrs. Sullivan, and out with the old, which would be *you*."

I shook my head slowly. "Still so childish,

Dean. And it's a pity because you were a good cop and could be a great chief. What's that saying about youth being wasted on the young? But last I heard, you're pushing the big four-oh. I believe that's considered middle-age now, isn't it?"

He reacted like I'd hit him below the belt, and maybe I had.

Three officers came out of the mansion. Two walked to one of the squad cars, without acknowledging either one of us, and got in and pulled away. The remaining one stood next to Bostwick. "Are we finished here, Chief?" he asked.

"Yeah, get in the car; I'll be right there."

"Look," I said, after the man was gone, "we both want to see this murder solved. It's your case, there's no arguing about that. You're in charge." When in doubt, stroke some ego.

Bostwick nodded.

"All I want to know is what evidence you have against Pierce to pin this on him. As far as I can see, there's just his lack of an alibi and the fact that a few witnesses saw him arguing with Stacey. Can you throw me a bone here? Maybe tell me what else you have?"

I don't know what I'd said that made his attitude soften a little, but he shrugged. "Look, if you can get Pierce to take a polygraph, maybe we can talk."

"Done. I know for a fact he has an alibi and a very reliable witness who'll back him up."

Bostwick's eyes lit up. "And who would that be?"

"You'll have to ask him."

When I got back into the jeep, Nathan didn't say a word. But halfway down the long driveway, his questions came tumbling out.

"So what did you say to him? It looked like you guys were going at it pretty good there for a while. Did he threaten you? Because if he did, I'll have a talk with him. Want me to talk to him for you? Are you okay, Kathy? Will you tell me what's going on?"

I had to laugh. "Calm down and give me a chance to answer."

He folded his hands and sat back in his seat. "Go ahead."

It took the entire drive back to tell him everything.

Because E.T. had driven Nathan and Brock to the diner, I was Nathan's ride home. Sully and I had spent many evenings playing cards or barbecuing with Nathan and Terry. They lived a few miles from my old neighborhood, and it felt like a strange homecoming when I parked on his street.

"I like the new paint job," I said, looking at his split-level ranch.

"I needed something to do . . . to get my mind off . . . you know . . . after Terry died."

"It's a nice shade of blue. Very soothing."

"That's what I thought." He started to unbuckle his seat belt. "You're coming in, aren't you?"

I looked at the clock on the dashboard, but it didn't matter what time it was. Lizzie and the kids weren't waiting for me. "Sure."

Rows of daffodils were lined up along either side of the front walk. Their bright yellow heads bobbed as we passed by, and I remembered how much Terry had loved them. I'd gone with her one time to the local garden center. She'd bought so many bags of bulbs that we'd had trouble fitting them all into the trunk of her compact car. As Nathan took out his keys, I stood there missing his wife—my friend.

He walked inside and then held the door open for me.

"Come on in."

Nothing had changed, except maybe the arrangement of the furniture, but even that wasn't drastic. Nathan's recliner had been moved closer to the TV, a new big screen. Terry's chair was still by the bookcase. Pictures of family and vacation spots still hung where they'd been for years. The worn couch had a new yellow throw draped across it with matching pillows at each end. I wondered if he'd picked them out or had someone help him.

"Get comfortable; I'll go grab a couple of beers. You still drink beer, don't you?"

"Have you met me?"

He left the room and I could hear him out in the kitchen opening cabinets and clanking glass. When he came back, he had a bottle in each hand and a bag of chips under one arm. He set a bottle on the table in front of me, tossed the bag down next to it, then collapsed in his big chair with his beer.

"Now," he started after I was done making noise opening the chip bag, "first thing you have to do is talk to Pierce about the polygraph."

"I already did. He and Lizzie will cooperate."

"Good deal."

"We should go back out to Buckhorn when we can take our time looking around without any interference," I said.

"I'm glad you said 'we' because there's no way you're going out there alone. After what happened to me, we know whoever it was is violent."

"I agree. And I've been thinking that I need to know more about Stacey Jordan. Maybe there's someone out there who isn't even connected to the whole Pierce art thing. Maybe her murder was personal."

"Like a jealous boyfriend or some coworker she pissed off?"

"We used to see that kind of thing all the time, remember?"

Nathan had a mouthful of chips and could only nod.

"Maybe an ex-lover tracked her down at the mansion. They were alone out there, no one to see. It would have been the perfect place to kill her."

After a long drink of beer, Nathan said, "I'll get Polly on that." Then casually he asked, "So what do you think of my crew?"

"They all seem more than competent. I especially like Rosie. She's a real character. And Polly sure knows her stuff. But E.T. . . . he's . . . an enigma."

"The guy drives me crazy with all his Zen-ness. I've seen him kick the crap out of a bad guy and the very next minute refuse to swat a fly. And you should see his apartment. Only the bare essentials. Nothing fancy like a TV or radio. And don't even get him started about the evils of a microwave. But when it comes down to weaponry and martial arts, he's a respected expert."

"Wouldn't it be funny to fix him up on a blind date with Lizzie?" I asked. The thought made me giggle.

"Stop laughing, they might surprise you and get along great. He's a pacifist who can be violent when he has to be. Elizabeth's a victim's advocate who can defend murderers if she has to. Each of them has a little bit of the old yin and yang inside of 'em."

"Maybe so."

"And good old Brock. He's a one-man army. You haven't had a chance to see him in action yet, but that big guy has the grace of a ballerina when he's pushed against the wall."

"I'll take your word for it."

Once the business part of our conversation was done, Nathan brought out an Al Pacino movie.

"I remember in our last e-mail that you mentioned wanting to see this. How about I run down to Chang's and bring back some lo mein; we can eat it while we watch."

I was touched that he'd gone out of his way for me. "Sounds perfect. I'll make some tea."

Chapter Twenty-Three

I hadn't packed anything appropriate for a walkathon. When I told Lizzie, she excitedly ran to get me a T-shirt listing sponsors down the back, including her office. My jeans would be fine, and I did have a pair of old sneakers I always traveled with.

I cleared away the breakfast dishes, since I was the first one dressed. Lizzie walked through the house, phone to her ear, giving her assistant Josh last minute instructions about what to bring to Westwood Park, where participants were scheduled to meet.

Chloe came up behind me. "Mom's on her phone twenty-four-seven. She practically sleeps with it. OMG, I was never that bad."

I turned around. "Chloe, sweetie, are you telling me that a grown-up woman, using a phone to run a business, support three people, pay bills, and arrange schedules, is the same as a teenager using her phone to ask a friend what she's wearing?"

She scrunched up her face. "I talk to my dad, too. That's important."

"I know it is. But I'm sure you can see it's not quite the same?"

Frustrated with my logic, she inhaled and blew out a long, frustrated sigh. "Guess not."

She'd managed to tie her short hair into a ponytail that stuck out of her head all bristly. Her face was scrubbed clean except for the pink lip gloss she loved to continually apply. An over-sized shirt hung loosely over her floral print leggings. Bright pink tennis shoes completed her ensemble.

I grabbed her and held on tight. "Do you have any idea how much I love you?" I asked.

"A lot," she mumbled into my chest.

When I finally released her, she burst out of my arms and ran for the door, shouting over her shoulder, "Love you, too!"

Lizzie came rushing in. "Can you help Cam get ready, Mother? I have to be there early to help set things up."

"Sure."

His door was open and I could see Cam sitting on the edge of the bed, dangling his bare feet.

"Put on your shoes and socks; we gotta get going."

"I'm working on something," he said, sketching on a large pad with a worn pencil.

"Can I see?"

"If you want. But I just started."

I walked into his cozy little room and sat next to him.

His hand moved swiftly across the rough paper

without a second of hesitation. What a contrast to the stiff, unsure way he carried himself. Watching him draw like that, it almost seemed as if he was taking directions from an inner voice.

The abstract shapes interconnected in a free-flowing, harmonious design. I felt a little envious of his innate talent. Nothing had ever come that easily to me. I'd always had to study and work so hard.

"I like it," I told him. "It makes me feel . . . peaceful."

"Me too."

"So what happened with your art project? Did the teacher like it?"

"I got a B plus. I would have gotten an A, but some glue from the frame leaked on a couple blocks." He pointed to the piece propped up on his desk.

He didn't seem to particularly care what his grade had been. But I still felt the need to cheer him on. It's what grandmothers do, I guess. "B plus is great. You should be proud."

Focused on his drawing, he didn't respond.

As I glanced over at the framed blocks, which had initially reminded me of Jackie's bracelet, I remembered Stacey had been wearing a similarly colorful one the day I met her at the gallery. Strange . . .

Lizzie suddenly appeared in the doorway.

"Come on, you two. We have to be there in twenty minutes."

Cameron got up off the bed carrying his pad and pencil to the computer desk in the corner.

With his back to us, he asked, "Do I have to walk at this thing . . . with all the other people? I don't know any of them."

Lizzie looked to me for some help.

"I'm not going to walk. You can sit with your old Grammy and watch. There'll be chairs or something, right?" I asked Lizzie.

"Bleachers are set up all along the course. And there should be refreshment stands so you can have a snack. Does that sound good, Cam?"

He turned around. "Will they have hot dogs?"

"Yep," his mother told him.

"Okay." He went to his dresser to find a pair of socks.

"I'll go get my jacket," I said as I started to leave the room.

"Grammy?"

"What, Cam?"

"You shouldn't call yourself old. 'Cause you're not."

"Thank you, Cam. I'll have to stop doing that."

The shirt Lizzie had given me was white with several puzzle pieces—the symbol for Autism Awareness—in the center. Each piece was a different color—red, yellow, and blue—and attendees' shirts, hats, visors, and jackets all featured at least one of these primary colors, making the park look like a gigantic field of tulips. The temperature had risen to seventy-five, adding to the crowd's enthusiasm.

Chloe perked up when she saw a few of her girlfriends and raced over to talk to them. Lizzie was immediately surrounded by volunteers needing direction. After assuring her I'd keep Cam close and Chloe well within sight, she hurried off, shouting her thanks as she went.

I scanned the crowd.

Margaret Ann stood with a few of her girls from the beauty shop. She waved, mouthing a hello. A young cop I'd worked with for a few months before I retired was with his family. I couldn't remember his name. He was holding a cooler while a woman I guessed to be his wife spread out a blanket on the lawn. It always threw me off seeing one of my men out of uniform in an unfamiliar setting. I knew them so well—and yet didn't.

Cam was quiet, as usual, and focused on the handheld game he'd brought from home. I led him through the crowd, looking for a space on the bleachers near the starting line.

"Katherine! Hey, Sullivan!"

I looked out over the crowd but couldn't see who had called me, so I sat. Cam plopped down next to me.

"Think you're too good to say hi to an old friend?"

I still couldn't figure out where the voice was coming from.

"Up here!"

Turning around, I saw Barbara Nylander sitting at the top of the bleachers.

"How long you been in town?" she asked, stepping down to sit beside me. "And why do I have to come all the way out here to see you?"

"I was planning to call you—swear—but I got involved in—"

"—the Jordan murder," she said, making sure Cam couldn't hear. "There are no secrets in this town, you know."

"It isn't a big secret. I'm just doing some investigating for Randolph Pierce's lawyer."

"Yeah, I heard your daughter hired you."

I had to laugh. "Nothing gets by you, does it?"

"Being the county coroner sort of puts me out there on the front line."

I wanted to ask a hundred questions and get her spin on the murder, but this wasn't the place. Cam had fooled me before into thinking he hadn't heard parts of a conversation, only to repeat every word that had been said later. Barbara was quick and caught on when I nodded toward him.

"We can talk business anytime," I said. "So how're you doing?"

"Better than the folks who end up on my table, that's for sure." She laughed at her own joke. She always did. Maybe it was her macabre sense of humor that helped her cope with what she had to do and see every day.

"How come you're not out there walking?" she asked. "You're in good shape."

"Oh, my grandson and I are spectators today. Right, Cam?" I turned to look at him but he never took his eyes off the game he held tightly.

"What about Elizabeth? Is she here?"

"Somewhere. She's one of the sponsors, which means she has to be everywhere at once. That's my granddaughter Chloe over there." I pointed.

"The one with the ponytail?"

"That's her."

"Cute."

"So are you going to walk today?" I asked.

"Bum knees, bad back. You know how it is. Once you hit fifty, everything starts to go."

"Must be hard with all the bending and standing you have to do on the job."

"Yeah it is, but I've only got a year and a half till retirement. Then John and I are heading south."

"Florida?"

"Hell's waiting room? God, no. I've seen enough old stiffs to last a lifetime. No, I've got a sister who lives in Rio; she runs a hotel down there. What a place. Gorgeous beaches, beautiful, healthy people. Emphasis on healthy." She laughed.

That time I did, too.

We tried to talk above the commotion around us, but it was getting frustrating.

Things were gearing up to start. I couldn't let Barbara get away. "You know, I'd like to stop by your office sometime."

"How about tomorrow?"

"Tomorrow's Sunday. Won't it be closed up?"

She winked. "I got the key. How's two o'clock? Gives me time to feed the old man and get him settled in front of the TV for his sport shows. He'll never miss me."

"I'll be there." I turned toward her, getting close to her ear. "This means a lot, thanks."

A voice came over the very loud speaker, first welcoming everyone, then thanking the crowd for their support. When a national representative started talking about what percentage of donations were going where, Cam reached over and shook my leg.

"Can we get hot dogs now?"

"Let's go."

Chapter Twenty~Four

Sunday afternoon at the county morgue—not exactly my idea of a good time. Barbara wore a white lab jacket over her pastel dress. She looked like a forensic church lady. "Prance on in here," she said when she saw me standing outside her office.

Born and raised on a ranch outside Dallas, she claimed that everything she knew about people had come from living around horses all her life. She had a theory that there were two kinds of body types in the world: racehorses and workhorses.

"Now, those models with their elongated necks and legs that go on for miles, they're racehorses. They're skittish and have to be handled with care. But workhorses are low to the ground and strong, determined hard workers. I'm a workhorse. What you see is what you get."

After reading her first two books on forensic techniques, I'd gone to a signing she was doing for her third. Before joining the force, I'd thought about being a forensics sketch artist and was eager to meet the intelligent, opinionated woman who had made such a name for herself in the male-dominated field.

We hit it off immediately. She, along with Sully,

encouraged me to join the force. And when I surprised everyone, mostly myself, with my interviewing technique, she told me to go that route instead of sketching. She'd started off as my mentor, and our friendship evolved from there. But we'd never visited each other's homes or celebrated one single holiday together. And after hundreds of coffee breaks and lunches shared in an office discussing a case, we agreed that keeping family separate from work was best for both of us.

"I got the report right here," she said, sitting behind her desk. "I just made a fresh pot of coffee. Want a cup?"

"No, I'm good."

"Well, I'm not. Would you pour me some?"

I walked to a small table where the coffee pot and cups were. A plate of shortbread cookies was next to the sugar.

"Can I have one of these?" I asked.

"Help yourself, darlin'."

I put her cup down in front of her and the cookie on the opposite side of her desk. Then I sat down.

"So fill me in on what y'all have so far," she said and leaned back to get comfortable.

I started from the beginning and didn't leave out a single detail. I ended by telling her about my conversation with Dean Bostwick in front of the mansion. As I rattled on, she sat stone-faced, listening intently, throwing in a nod here and there. When I was finally finished, she nodded some more.

Then she said, "You certainly have been a busy girl, haven't you?"

"I sure have."

"So tell me, how well did you know Stacey?"

"I know she worked for Randolph Pierce at his gallery and with Antoine Rousseau at the estate. She had an art degree. I only met her once but remember she was pretty and intelligent. But I'll tell you, Barb, everyday seems to bring more surprises to this case. I was hoping you'd have some information that might help me."

Barbara opened the white manila file. "Well, here's what I know: Stacey Jordan, Caucasian female, twenty-eight years of age. Five feet, six inches tall, one hundred and ten pounds. Healthy, no diseases, no scars, no evidence of ever giving birth. From the ID police found in her wallet, she lived in Minneapolis at five-oh-six Walnut."

"And what was the official cause of death?" I asked.

"Blunt force trauma. A pattern mark in the center of the back of her skull suggested a heavy round object was used, approximately the size of a tennis ball. She was struck three times. The first blow didn't kill her, probably just knocked her unconscious. This caused her to fall forward, hitting her forehead pretty good but not hard enough to kill her. The second strike did the trick. I picked out some metallic flecks from the wound, which, when tested, turned out to be a gold overlay of some sort. There was no DNA or skin in the wound other than Stacey's. Nothing was found under her fingernails. She couldn't have put up a fight—"

"—because she was attacked from behind," I finished. "Can you tell the approximate height of the killer from the angle of the blows?"

"If there had been only one, I could. But the other two strikes opened up the area more."

"How many assailants do you think there were?"

"Only one. I'm positive about that."

"And what do you make of those scratches along her arms?"

"I'd say that whoever killed her tried to move the body, probably to hide it. She was dead when she was scratched."

"That's what I thought."

Barbara put the file down. "Such a shame. From what I heard, Stacey's only relative was her mother. But the poor woman's very ill—cancer. And we can't release the body to her until we're finished with the case."

All I could do was shake my head. Then I remembered something. "Could the metallic head of a walking stick be the murder weapon?"

"Well, theoretically, anything can be a murder weapon. It all depends upon the force of the blow. Why?"

"Someone I know carries a cane with a head about that size," I said.

"If you bring it in, I can examine it for trace evidence."

"Thanks so much. And how long ago did Bostwick receive your report?" I asked.

Barbara leaned forward, making her chair squeak. "Oh, he hasn't gotten it yet."

I stopped wiping cookie crumbs off my fingers. "You mean . . . ?"

"Y'all are the first to see this report, besides me, of course."

I tried, but I couldn't keep the corners of my mouth from curling up into a big grin.

"This paperwork gets sent to his office tomorrow. So let's keep this between us fillies for now."

"Of course. But how did you know I'd want to see your report in the first place?"

"Oh, I wasn't sure. But when I heard you were investigating the murder, I had a good hunch. You know, Katie, ever since you left the force, I've become Bostwick's target. I can't, for the life of me, figure out why he has it in for us old broads. Maybe it's a mother issue or some such nonsense as that. But whatever it is, I just wanted to make his job a little bit more . . . challenging. Know what I mean?"

I knew exactly what she meant.

Chapter Twenty~Five

When I got back in the jeep, I called Nathan and told him what I had learned from Barbara. I'd been thinking that a background check on Stacey would be helpful. He said Polly was the one to go to and that she was planning to paint her kitchen and would be home all weekend. He gave me her number. I called her and she said she was ready for a break, so I headed right over.

Before ringing the bell, I noticed the name above it read Pauline Mercer. Somehow, not knowing Polly's real name made me feel embarrassed that I had come to her home needing a favor. I wondered what I should call her. Polly or Pauline?

People have always told me I think too much. How can that be? Isn't thinking a good thing? Isn't that what separates us from trees . . . and rocks? But maybe in this case, they were right. After a moment, I decided that if she was good with her nickname, then so was I.

She buzzed me up to the third floor and was standing, holding the door of her apartment open, when I arrived.

"Hey, Katherine."

"Hey, Polly, sorry to bother you on a Sunday."

"No biggie."

She let me into the apartment and my nose was immediately hit with the smell of paint fumes.

"I turned on a fan; hope it helps." She was wearing ripped jeans and a black smock, both spattered with the dark purple she was painting the kitchen. An interesting choice, I thought.

"It's fine." Truth is I like the smell of paint.

Her living room had been turned into an office. Four computers sat on four separate tables, which had been pushed up against their own wall. Each had a chair in front of it.

"Sorry there's no comfortable place to sit. I don't usually have guests."

"A chair is fine."

"So Nathan called after he hung up with you. He said something about doing a background check on Stacey Jordan?"

"If it wouldn't be too much trouble?"

"No trouble. It shouldn't take that long."

She walked to the largest computer, sat down, and started typing. Her fingers ran across the keyboard gracefully. After asking for the correct spelling of Stacey's name and a current address, the only sound in the room was the clicking of the keyboard.

It only took about ten minutes. And then she said, "Here it is. Pull your chair closer."

"Wow. Are those all her debts?" I asked.

"Thirteen whole pages of 'em," she said.

"Twenty thousand in student loans. A car loan from three years ago. Jewelry and looks like . . . about thirty thousand in credit cards."

"So we can rule out anyone killing her for her money."

Polly chuckled. "For sure. No insurance policies either."

"What about relatives or a husband?" I asked.

"No husband, no divorces, no children. One sister, deceased two years ago. Nothing here about a father. But her mother's alive and . . . not well."

"Yeah, I think she has cancer."

"That would explain all the doctor bills. She owes two oncologists big time."

"Was she ever arrested?" I asked.

A few more clicks of the keyboard. "Once for shoplifting. But that was years ago. Nothing since."

"So the only other name I've added to my list is her mother, who would be . . . how old?"

It was miraculous how quickly Polly was able to come up with the information. Miraculous and a little scary. Knowing that my personal information was out there like Ms. Jordan's was made me feel vulnerable.

"Her mother, Nancy Jordan, is . . . fifty-three."

I tried not thinking about how much older I was than the poor woman or how devastated I'd be if anything ever happened to my daughter.

"Want a peek at her bank records?" Polly asked.

"You can get to them? I thought there were all sorts of safeguards."

"Here we go. The Mercantile in Minneapolis." Polly scrolled down, looking at monthly balances. "Nothing unusual. Two insufficient fund notices last year but she worked consistently. Wow, look at this." She pointed to the screen.

I scooched closer, promising myself to buy an extra pair of reading glasses.

"Look at this deposit," she said. "For months it's always the same. Every Friday, she takes her paycheck from the art museum where she works and deposits it into her account. Seven hundred and fifty dollars deposited like clockwork. And then this."

I squinted. "Five thousand from . . ."

Polly clicked onto Stacey's balance and brought up a direct deposit from the L'Etoile du Nord Foundation. "There's another one a month later for seven thousand, five hundred, and just before she died, ten thousand, three hundred. All from this foundation."

"Is there an address on the checks?" I asked.

"No, it just says: L'Etoile du Nord. Huh, wonder what that means."

"The Star of the North," I said. "It's the state motto of Minnesota."

"Why's it in French?" Polly asked.

"Something about the French explorers . . . I

forget exactly. We had to learn all that in school. And that was a long time ago." French made me think of Antoine Rousseau. Could he be involved in Stacey's murder?

"So now what?" Polly asked.

"I think I'm going to Minneapolis," I said, still unsure what was going on.

"You better not go alone. If I was you, I'd take Brock with me. You'll have to feed him, but he's as tough as they come. He'll keep you safe."

"Why do you think I need protection?"

"Come on, Kate, we're talking murder here." She looked at me like I wasn't understanding the situation fully. "I know you were a police chief and all that. You've had some training and can handle yourself. But it never hurts to bring along some backup, right?"

"Right."

When I stood to leave, a little dog came around the corner from what I assumed was a bedroom. He looked like a cross between cocker spaniel and poodle. After sniffing my shoes, he jumped up on Polly's lap.

"This is Herbie," she said, petting the animal. "I grabbed him during a raid we did on a testing lab."

Herbie licked Polly's face. For a minute, the two seemed oblivious that I was there. Nathan told me once that Polly wasn't big on people and preferred being alone with her machines and animals. It sure looked like that was true.

"Well, I'll let you get back to your painting. I've bothered you enough for one day." Leaning over, I scratched the dog behind his ear.

Showing his teeth, he growled.

"Strangers still scare him. It'll take a while until he trusts people again."

"But he sure loves you." I walked to the door. "Thanks again, Polly."

She didn't get up, just waved. "Anytime."

Chapter Twenty~Six

After visiting Polly, I went back to the house. Lizzie was setting the table. Sunday dinner was the one meal a week she always made a point of fussing over. I went to help her.

Conversation around the table was lively. Yesterday's walkathon had been a big success. Lizzie was bursting to tell me about all the money they'd raised and how it would be distributed. Chloe couldn't stop talking about a boy in her class who happened to turn up at the event.

"All the girls like him but I think he likes me best. Can you believe it? He's got blond hair and these deep dimples in his cheeks." She hesitated to smile. "Wouldn't it be cray-cray if I got a real boyfriend this semester?"

Lizzie and I didn't discourage her by saying she was too young for a boyfriend. Or explain that maybe she was reading him wrong. We both understood her feelings and just enjoyed the moment, watching her be so happy.

Cam sat quietly, eating his pot roast, content. I've learned a lot about the value of quiet observation from my grandson. The ability to absorb my surroundings instead of gloss over small details has helped me in my work and art.

Then it was my turn. All of them wanted to know what I'd done that day. Where had I gone? Who had I seen?

I talked in generalizations. Told the kids about my illustrious friend, Barbara, and how I'd gone to her office just to say hi. I went out of my way not to mention that her office was in the morgue. I told them we had fun catching up. But I never threw in the fact that we'd been discussing a murder. For good measure, I told them about visiting Nathan's friend, Polly. The three of them listened politely but never asked a single question—until I mentioned Herbie. Of course, I didn't tell them how Polly came to have Herbie.

While the kids begged their mother for a dog, which they did weekly, I noticed how Lizzie avoided making eye contact with me. We hadn't had time alone to discuss my last visit to the jail. She knew I'd left the building hurt and angry. And we both knew we'd make the time to talk things out later.

Chloe and Cam had been in bed about an hour when Lizzie and I gravitated to the comfortable sofa in the family room, on the other side of the house.

She rubbed her palms together, a nervous habit she seemed to have acquired since quitting the law firm. It became more pronounced when she was frustrated. I really hadn't noticed it until recently.

"I am so sorry, Mother. About everything. I never set out to intentionally lie to you. Randy and I were still so new, just trying to figure out how we felt about each other that night. It was private, just between the two of us. Then Stacey got murdered, and Randy was hauled in for questioning. He was only trying to protect me, but when he got thrown in jail . . . everything got so complicated and we didn't know how to get out of the lie."

"So you hired me to prove him innocent."

"Yes."

"Well. I'm still angry about the whole thing. And you being a lawyer should have known better. I hate that you're involved in this."

"I know, I know. I should have said something right away."

"You both should have," I said.

She looked at me, then really looked at me, and asked, "Do you know how much longer you'll be mad at me?"

At that moment, my forgiveness was the only thing that could make her feel better. And how often can a problem be solved with just a hug? So I moved closer. She cried into my shoulder when we made contact.

"Until . . . tomorrow. I'm going to be mad at

you until breakfast tomorrow. That's the best I can do."

That made her laugh. She sat up and wiped at her tears with both hands. "I'll take it."

After we both calmed down, I asked, "So, what about Randolph giving up his DNA and taking the polygraph?" I knew there was no DNA left at the scene, but I didn't want to tell her that until Randolph gave his sample.

"I'm going down there tomorrow to arrange everything," she said. "Randolph agreed to tell the truth about where he was that night."

"Good. And you?"

"I'll take a polygraph, too. When Dean sees that my test corroborates Randolph's alibi, he'll have to release him."

"Then you'll have no reason to represent him. And when Bostwick asks why the change of heart, you'll have to come up with something that'll satisfy him."

"I think the truth should do it. He has to understand we were both concerned with our professional reputations."

"What about your personal one?"

She shrugged off my question. "Oh, who cares about that anymore?"

"You're being a little naïve here, Lizzie. You were born and raised in this town. You've set up practice here; your children go to school here."

"Maybe there'll be talk for a while—until

people get bored and move on to another scandal."

My beautiful daughter lived by the rules and it had always paid off for her. She'd married well, bought a home in an upscale neighborhood. She paid her taxes on time, never jaywalked, and gave to charity. But working as a criminal defense attorney had brought death threats in the mail. She'd gotten up close and personal with far too many bad guys. And when Cam was born with Asperger's, she'd watched him being bullied and stared at. So how then could she not understand the repercussions of her actions? I was dumb-founded.

"It's human nature to gossip; people relish knowing that their neighbor is more miserable than they are. And if you think the Internet is bad, you should have been a mother before PCs. We didn't have Facebook or Twitter, but we had backyard fences and the grocery store. Not to mention good old-fashioned phones in our house where we could have a private conversation—in private—not out on the street for every pedestrian to hear. It was just as bad back then, believe me."

"Don't worry, Mother. I'll watch myself."

"So if Randolph's released and you no longer represent him, I guess there's no reason for me to continue my investigation," I said.

"He'll need a lawyer until this is all over. We've

both seen cases where the accused passes the lie detector and still ends up in jail. So please—for me—stay and find the real killer so we can all get back to normal."

"All right, I'll stay . . . but I'm not sure about the normal part." I laughed, but I wasn't kidding.

Without the kids around, I was able to fill her in on the details of my day, especially what I'd learned about Stacey's finances.

"So what's your next move?" Lizzie asked.

"I think I'm going to Minneapolis."

Chapter Twenty~Seven

Despite what I had told Polly, I'd planned to drive up to Minneapolis alone but made the mistake of calling Nathan before I left.

"I can't get away from the office today but—"

"Come on, Nathan, I can make a twenty-minute drive by myself."

"Polly told me all about the bank statements and Stacey's mother. She said she suggested you take Brock along with you."

"I don't need a bodyguard. And please stop treating me like I'm helpless."

"If you think that I think you're helpless, you're nuts. But in the few years you've been retired, a lot has changed, Kathy. If you look sideways at someone now, they're liable to pull a gun."

"Unless Brock's Superman, I don't think he can stop a bullet—"

"Kathy! Please . . . for me. All you have to do is feed the big guy. He'll sit in the car and mind his own business. But if you need help—"

"All right . . . all right. Where should I pick him up?"

"Hey, Mrs. Sullivan." Brock opened the door and climbed into the Cherokee. As he fastened his seat belt, I noticed how much room he took up in the vehicle.

"I thought I told you to call me Katherine." I smiled.

"You got it."

"I guess Nathan told you why I'm going to Minneapolis?" I asked.

"No. He just said you might need some . . . help."

Brock stared straight ahead, no expression on his face. Because it was a warm day, he'd worn a short sleeve polo shirt, which accentuated his muscles. Out of the corner of my eye, I could see his arms were covered with tattoos: animals, random words, numbers, and initials. His brown hair had been buzzed, his skin was tan, and I'd describe him as a handsome man.

We drove in silence. He looked out his side window now and then. I concentrated on the road ahead. But after I'd merged onto 100N, the silence in the jeep was making me uncomfortable.

Strong silent types have always made me work extra hard at a conversation.

Finally I thought of something sure to engage him. "Nathan said I had to feed you when we finish up at Stacey's." I laughed. "Anything special you'd like for lunch?"

"Well there's this new place—I wrote down the address." He actually seemed excited.

"What's it called?"

He pulled a piece of paper out of the back pocket of his jeans. "It's called Bouillabaisse. Chef Roberts, he's from France, opened it a month ago. I hear nice things."

It's the little surprises that make life so much fun. "Bouillabaisse—that's the French name for a fish stew. You like French cooking?"

"Love it. The things they know about sauces are unbelievable."

"Do you cook?" I asked.

"I take classes here and there. But don't tell the crew. They'd never let me hear the end of it."

"Our secret . . . promise."

"My dad owned a greasy spoon in St. Paul. I helped out every chance I could. Weekends, holidays, summer vacation. When he died, I helped my mother run the place . . . until she died. My brother never had no interest, so we sold it and split the cash. He bought a house with his share; I put my half in the bank."

"Very sensible," I said. "But you have to spend some of it on yourself—have some fun."

"Oh, I take out a bunch when I want to travel. I been to New York, Vegas last year, and I'm goin' to New Orleans this year. I can hardly wait to see what's goin' on in NOLA. That's Emeril's place in the Quarter." He stopped. "Am I boring you with all this stuff?"

"Not at all. It's fun finding new places and foods."

"It's what life's all about, ain't it?"

"So would I be surprised to see what's in your kitchen?"

"For sure. Next time I make up a batch of dad's barbeque sauce, you'll come over for ribs."

Who would have thought that Brock and I would have cooking in common?

The turnoff for Olson Memorial Highway came up much too soon.

But all the fun came to a screeching halt when I parked in front of Stacey's small house.

"I assumed she lived in an apartment and that I'd talk the manager into letting us in, but now . . ."

"You know, most people really do keep a spare key under a welcome mat or flower pot. Even those phony plastic rocks. Like they're really foolin' someone. Let's go have a look."

"It's worth a try," I said. "But act as though we belong here. If you look confident, you can get away with a whole lot."

We got out of the jeep and calmly walked toward the house. I'd learned that Mondays and Tuesdays are always the best days of the week to do anything. Stores are empty after the weekend rush, and there's less traffic because drivers are at work, school, or home. Stacey's neighborhood was no exception. There was not one person as far as I could see, on either side of the street.

Brock led the way up the two steps to the porch and twisted the doorknob, checking to see if it was unlocked. No such luck.

I bent down and lifted the monogrammed mat. No key there.

A large plant in a stone planter sat by the front door. Before I could ask, Brock picked it up. If I couldn't lift the pot, I doubted Stacey could have.

The key was there.

Seeing my surprise, Brock said, "It ain't as heavy as it looks."

We unlocked the door and walked inside.

Chapter Twenty-Eight

It's standard procedure for police to check out the home of a murder victim. And if the victim was connected to other crimes or associated with criminals, then the search is a thorough one. But Stacey Jordan had been an ordinary citizen, living an ordinary life.

"Looks pretty clean," Brock said.

A pile of magazines by a chair had been knocked over and was spread across the floor. A few pillows were lying in a heap on top of a floral print sofa.

"The police have obviously been through here, though," I said.

Brock stood in the middle of the room, his hands deep in his pockets. "She sure has a lot of pictures."

I turned to see what he was staring at. Two rows of framed prints had been positioned at eye level all around the room. Rembrandts next to Picassos, Rockwells alongside classics. I wondered if there was any sort of order to the seemingly haphazard arrangement.

"Are they real?" Brock asked.

"No. Just copies."

"I really like that one." He pointed.

I stepped in closer. "That's a marriage series by

Zeng Fanzhi. It sold for more than six million."

"Wow! Ain't artists supposed to be struggling? You know, livin' in tiny rooms in Paris . . . or crazy an' cutting off an ear?"

I laughed. "Well nowadays modern art is a big commodity. A lot of artists are beyond rich."

"Reminds me of *Star Wars*," he said, looking at a larger piece.

"Glenn Brown. He does sci-fi paintings."

Brock shrugged. "I shoulda paid more attention in third grade when Miss Dale was teachin' us art."

I started to walk toward a hallway.

"Wait for me," he said. "You never know what's around the corner."

I slowed my pace . . . a little.

There was one large bedroom to the right of the hall. Across from that was a small bathroom, and straight ahead, the kitchen. I turned toward the bedroom.

"Don't touch anything," I told him out of reflex. "We have to be careful. No telling if something might lead back here."

"Understood," Brock said seriously.

Several dresser drawers were open. Either Stacey had left them that way or the police had. I walked over and glanced inside. One was filled with lingerie and the other with socks.

The room was decorated in an art deco style, very feminine. Cosmetics and perfume bottles were scattered along the surface of the largest dresser. The smaller one had a black lacquered jewelry box on top of it. Her satin bedspread had been turned back. Again, I couldn't know if the police or Stacey were responsible.

"Same stuff in here," Brock said.

When I looked at him, he made a circular motion with his hands indicating the walls.

More artwork, but in the bedroom, it had been coordinated with the décor. Ertes and Mucha posters, most featuring beautiful women in beautiful gowns. There was no desk, no TV.

We glanced in the bathroom. Brock took a towel off the rack, wrapped his hand with it, then switched on the overhead light.

"Everything's in its place, I guess," he said.

"Look behind the shower curtain," I told him.

The big man walked further into the room, making it look miniature. Reaching, he pulled the curtain aside. For a brief—very brief— second, I expected someone to be hiding there and held my breath. But there was just a tub, a shower head, and two bottles of shampoo on a plastic shelf.

"Let's look in the kitchen," I told him.

Brock flipped the bathroom lights off and then hung up the towel, ever so neatly. The care he took surprised me.

The kitchen was bright and neat. I could see that the police had moved a canister out of its place. The silverware drawer was open. No dirty dishes in the sink. I pulled my sleeve down to cover my hand and opened the refrigerator. Nothing in there except a carton of milk, strawberry yogurt, and butter. I was tempted to throw out the milk and yogurt before they could spoil but resisted.

"Guess this was a waste of time," I said.

"So are we gonna go now?"

"One last look at her desk."

We left the kitchen, went back down the hall, and stopped in front of Stacey's desk in the living room. I hadn't noticed it the first time, but there was a large coffee-table book lying facedown to the right of where the computer had been. I took a tissue from the decorative box on the desk, covered my fingers, and lifted it up. It was *The Life and Art of Gustav Klimt*. Then, taking another tissue, I opened the drawers of the desk, starting with the small middle one, ending with the large bottom one on the right.

Inside was just the usual: fresh paper; printer cartridges; manuals for the computer and a tablet, which the police probably took; paper clips; pens; rubber bands; blank note pads.

Then it hit me. The cookbooks on a top shelf in the kitchen hadn't looked right. I hurried back there with Brock trailing behind.

Pointing, I asked him, "See that thin black book? Could you please take it down?"

Brock reached up, removed the book, and held it out to me.

My first instinct was to grab it, have a good look. But my training had taught me to fight impulsive moves and slow down. So I did.

"I knew this wasn't a cookbook. All the other spines are so colorful. This one just didn't belong."

"I don't get it. What is it?" Brock asked.

"We're going to find out."

I laid the slim black book on top of the kitchen table, opening it to the first page.

It was a notebook filled with names of people I didn't recognize, beneath each name an address. All sorts of numbers, probably connected to phones and computers. Beside each name was what looked like a code number and a dollar amount. As I leafed through, I counted five pages filled from top to bottom, dating from February 10, 2012, to the present.

"Whatever it is, she was smart enough to go the old fashion route and write everything down. No chance of getting hacked or having anything deleted."

I carefully tucked the book into a plastic sandwich bag I found in the kitchen and then closed all the desk drawers. "Now we can go."

Brock looked down at his watch. "Perfect timing for lunch."

Chapter Twenty-Nine

Eating lunch at a French restaurant with Brock was an entirely different experience than eating at the diner in Edina had been. He was warm and interesting, so knowledgeable about food and cooking. We took in the ambiance as well as the décor, which Brock explained to me are two different things. One refers is the actual decorations on the wall and the other to the way a room makes you feel while you're inside it.

Brock thought his bouillabaisse was under-seasoned; I thought my salade Niçoise was exceptional. We taste tested each other's entrée and rated them as if we were food critics writing a review.

Afterward, while we waited for the check, I took out my phone and searched for the location of a Mercantile Bank closest to Stacey's home. I figured she'd use the most convenient branch and hopefully one of the tellers or a manager knew her personally. There were four around town, one about a mile from her place. I dialed and asked for a manager to inform them that I'd be coming in on official business, investigating the murder of Stacey Jordan. The woman I spoke to, Ms. Price, told me how shocked she'd been hearing the news and would cooperate with me completely. I told her I'd be there in fifteen minutes.

"Good news?" Brock asked, seeing my smile.

"No, good luck. What are the odds of me finding someone who knew Stacey on my first try?"

"Ahhh, I don't know; I ain't so good with numbers."

"That's okay."

When he reached for the check, I grabbed his hand. "This is business." Then I handed the waiter my Visa card.

The nameplate on her desk said she was Cynthia Price, Account Manager. She was an older woman, somewhere in her fifties. She had dark, shoulder-length hair, with gray streaks running through it. Her eyebrows had been penciled in and made her look surprised. Her lipstick was a deep red; her clothes were business drab.

"Mrs. Sullivan, please have a seat."

"Thanks for seeing me."

"Anything I can do to help find the dreadful person who killed Stacey—just ask." She gritted her teeth and I could see how difficult this was for her.

I outlined the case, mentioning that I'd found Stacey's bank statements among her personal belongings. If I'd told her how Polly had hacked into their system, I was sure she would have been less . . . cordial.

"I was hoping," I started gently, "that maybe you could tell me something about Stacey on a more personal level. I only met her once and we talked for a very brief time. It's probably a long shot but I don't know any of her friends. Maybe you can tell me something . . . anything?"

Mrs. Price thought for a moment. "Well . . . let me see. I was the one who set up her checking and savings accounts. That was on," she leaned forward and looked at her computer screen, "October sixteenth, two thousand ten. At the time, she was working at the Miller Art Center over on Hennepin. Are you familiar with it?"

I nodded. "Oh yes, I've spent many hours there."

"It is a beautiful place." Then I lost her a moment while she reflected on a memory. "There was something about Stacey. She reminded me of my daughter." Mrs. Price glanced over at the photo of a beautiful young woman hanging on the wall behind her. "Nina's always been so enthusiastic about everything. That's the way Stacey was, too. It was lovely to see how much they each enjoyed their jobs . . . just life in general, you know? Nina and I used to love to tour the museums together. We had so many wonderful times. But when she moved to LA, I stopped going."

"What a shame. I traipse all over the place by myself. The first few times were uncomfortable but then it all became an adventure."

"Oh no, I could never do that."

"Did you ever go with Stacey?" I asked.

"No, I'm afraid we didn't have that kind of friendship. We never saw each other outside of the bank."

"Would you happen to know where her mother lives?"

"Mrs. Davidson? She's at the Palmer House Apartments, downtown on Fifth."

"Oh, I know exactly where that is."

"I can't imagine losing a daughter." She wiped away a tear and seemed embarrassed by her display of emotion.

"When was the last time you saw her?"

"The Thursday before she . . . passed."

"What was her mood like?" I asked.

"She wasn't her usual peppy self. She said she was just very tired."

"The L'Etoile du Nord company. Seems that Stacey received some large checks from them."

"Let's have a look." Ms. Price started working the keyboard in front of her computer. While she typed, she said, "I do remember Stacey telling me it was a charitable foundation she worked with on occasion. She said they had set up a school and several orphanages. Here it is. Their account's out of a New York bank. The last deposit was a month ago, on the tenth." She looked up at me. "I can't give you any more information than that. I mean, you're not the police . . ."

I wrote down the date. "I understand. But can you by any chance tell me the exact number of checks she received from them?"

"Sure." A few clicks. "Only three, all within the last year. But that's all I can say."

This woman was beyond helpful. "I don't know how to thank you."

"Just catch the monster. And I'm hoping there'll be a service or memorial for her? If you find out anything, could you please let me know?" She handed me her card. "Some of the other girls would like to attend as well."

"I'll definitely do that."

Chapter Thirty

"How'd it go?" Brock asked as I started the engine.

"Better than I expected."

"So the bank lady told you some stuff about Ms. Jordan?"

"Seems she thought of Stacey as a daughter. Her murder hit her pretty hard."

"The boss called while you were inside. He says he couldn't get a hold of you."

"I wish he'd stop being such a—"

"He's just worried about you, that's all."

"I know."

"And as long as you keep investigatin' and the killer's still out there, you're gonna run into him sooner or later. That's all I'm sayin'. Neither one of us wants you to get hurt."

As we came to a stoplight, I turned to Brock. "Thanks."

"So are we goin' home now or what?" he asked.

"No, we've got one more stop."

The Palmer House Apartments was a retirement home unlike any I had seen before. Situated on a street corner in a gentrified section of downtown, it looked more like an upscale hotel. Beneath a green awning stood a doorman wearing a red jacket with shiny gold buttons. While Brock waited in the car, I walked into the lobby, where a security guard called upstairs to announce me before directing me to her room.

I took the elevator to the eighth floor and knocked on the door. A nurse in a white uniform answered.

"Are you Mrs. Sullivan?"

"Yes. Is Mrs. Davidson feeling well enough to talk?"

"About what?"

"I'm investigating the death of her daughter and was hoping she might have some information that would help me."

The nurse shook her head. "Don't you think this is too soon to be interrogating the poor woman? Besides, I saw in the news that the killer's already been arrested."

"There's a man being held but he hasn't been formally charged, yet."

From just inside the apartment, a woman's voice called out weakly, "For Pete's sake, Josephine, let her in!"

Meekly, the nurse stepped aside and held the door open for me.

The woman I saw sitting on the couch looked to be in good health. She was rosy cheeked and had a full head of grey hair.

She waved at me and said, "Come in, dear. Sit down. Can I have Josephine get you some tea?"

"No, no, I'm not going to bother you for long. I just have a few questions."

"I can't tell you how grateful I am that you're investigating my daughter's death but I read that the killer's already been caught. It's that Randolph Pierce, the man she worked for in Edina . . . isn't it?"

"Mr. Pierce claims that he's innocent and has hired me to find the real killer. Besides," I said, repeating myself, "he hasn't been charged, yet."

"Oh, my. Well, anything I can do to help. I certainly don't want the wrong person to pay for my daughter's death."

"Did your daughter feel threatened while she was working for the Pierce family?"

"Well, I can tell you she and Mr. Pierce butted heads often. For some reason, he thought she was going to write a tell-all book. And you know how that family loves their secrets. But Stacey wasn't afraid, if that's what you mean."

"Can you tell me anything about her association with a man named Antoine Rousseau?"

"You mean the Frenchman? All I know about him is that he was a perfectionist and was very generous to her."

We talked a bit more about her friends, ex-boyfriends, and possible enemies, but her mother would just smile and say, "Everybody loved my Stacey."

I felt the nurse's hand on my shoulder from

behind. "She's getting tired. Maybe it's time for you to leave."

We said our good-byes and she invited me to come and see her again. On the way to the door, I looked around and asked Josephine, "Was Stacey paying for all this, or is there insurance?"

"Only Medicare, but her medical bills are astronomical. Her daughter was an angel and paid for everything else. I don't know where she got the money, but she told me not to worry—in the art community, there's plenty of money to go around."

"She didn't tell you where the money was coming from?"

"She'd recently started working at the Pierce estate and at his gallery as well. I tried telling her she was spreading herself too thin, but she kept saying she needed the money for her mother. I assumed she was being paid very well."

"Did she talk to you about Randolph Pierce? Or Antoine Rousseau?"

"A little."

I tried not to look too anxious. "Did she say anything about having an argument with Mr. Pierce?"

"There wasn't just one. She told her mother he was an arrogant egotist."

"And what did she say about Mr. Rousseau?"

"She liked him better than Mr. Pierce." Josephine laughed to herself. "At first she was impressed with his credentials, and the fact that he was a Frenchman seemed to sort of excite her. She thought he was very . . . continental. That was the exact word she used. But then, after a while, she found his obsessive-compulsiveness to be unbearable. Everything had to be perfect. His suits, his hair, even Stacey's clothes. That man drove her crazy."

"Yes, I've met him. He is very fastidious. The last time I saw him, he was standing outside a gallery in the middle of the day and looked like he was going to a formal dinner."

"He must be loaded. The money he's spent on his art collection—"

"He has a private collection?"

"Oh yes. He swore Stacey to secrecy. Told her that he's dedicated his life to tracking down specific pieces. One time, he was working on the restoration of a villa in Spain. He heard that a Goya he'd been looking for since the nineties had been discovered, and he took off. He spent the next few months tracking it down and finally convinced the owner to sell."

"Do you mind if I take notes?" I asked.

"Not at all. I'm not telling you anything that I wouldn't tell the police if they asked. But no one's been around to ask a single thing about that beautiful girl."

I took my note pad out of my purse. Now that I was getting new information, I couldn't afford to forget a single bit of it.

• • •

"Any luck?" Brock asked as I got back into the car.

"Let's head home. I'll tell you along the way."

Brock looked at his watch. "Do you think we'll make it in time for my six o'clock workout?"

"Traffic seems to be moving well. I don't see why not."

After dropping Brock off, I pulled over and called Dean Bostwick. He was out of the office but the officer on duty gave me his cell number.

"Bostwick here."

"Dean, it's Katherine Sullivan."

"I was wondering why I didn't recognize the number."

"Have you talked to Randolph Pierce today?"

"Right after he took the polygraph. I don't know how you did it but . . . it was a big help."

"And the DNA?"

"Oh, he gave that up, too. We even hooked up his lawyer—your daughter. Both parties couldn't have been more cooperative."

"And?" I hated that he made me ask.

"They passed with flying colors. But I have to tell you, I was surprised that your daughter was his alibi—"

"So when do you release Randolph?"

"He's still our number-one suspect. So I'm holding him until I'm one hundred percent satisfied that he's innocent."

"But he passed the polygraph."

"Come on, Katherine, you know those machines and tests aren't perfect."

"But you can't just continue to hold him without charging him."

"You want me to charge him?"

"That's not my point. Even a seventy-two-hour hold would be up by now."

"Let's say I'm keeping him in protective custody, at least until the DNA test comes back."

"Protecting him from what?"

"Taking off!"

It seemed the wheels of justice moved slower with the introduction of each new technique instead of speeding up. Some still claimed that DNA testing was junk science.

"But you still owe me," I said. "You agreed to share information if I got Pierce to take the test. Can we meet in your office tomorrow?"

I expected him to start handing me excuses but he didn't. Instead he said, "How's two o'clock?"

"I'll be there."

After hanging up, I called Lizzie to tell her I wouldn't be home for dinner and drove to Nathan's office.

"Knock, knock."

"Hey!" he said looking up from his desk.

"What kind of a security business doesn't have a system wired up in their own office? There was no one out front and I just walked in. I could have been a serial killer, a burglar, or a—"

"Okay, I get it. The damn thing just quit today. It should be up and running tomorrow."

I couldn't let it go. Not after he'd insisted I take Brock along with me for protection. "Tomorrow isn't today . . . now is it?"

Nathan came around his desk, laughing. "Enough already." Then he hugged me. "It's good to see you, even if you just came to chew me out."

"No, I'm here to discuss this case with you. The fact that I got to lecture a security expert about security was just an added bonus."

"So should we talk here or over dinner?"

"Please—no more food today. Brock and I had a big lunch; I'm still full."

"That boy can sure put it away, can't he?"

I decided not to tell Nathan that Brock was a foodie. It made me feel that I'd bonded with the big guy in a way no one else in the office had. "Let's talk here, but I will take a Coke from that machine over there . . . please."

"You got it. Make yourself comfortable."

I hooked my purse on the coatrack in the corner, unzipped my jacket, and hung that up, too. It had been a long day, and at that moment, I was uncomfortable in my clothes and skin. The collar of my blouse felt restricting, the button on my jeans pulled, and my new shoes had rubbed blisters. I dragged a second chair over and put my feet up.

Nathan walked into the room with a Coke in each hand, and when he saw me like that, he chuckled. "This getting old crap is for the birds, isn't it? I swear every day there's another ache in another region of my body."

"Lizzie and the kids never give me a free pass when I complain and I'm not giving you one. If you think old, you are old."

He handed me the soda. "You try being around all these young folks. It just gets to me sometimes."

"Well we can grumble amongst ourselves, but we can't let the youngsters see us sweat."

"I hear that."

We relaxed a minute before he started.

"So what happened in Minneapolis?"

I told him about going to Stacey's house. It really wasn't breaking and entering if we had a key. Right? I could tell Nathan didn't agree with my logic, but he kept his opinion to himself and just nodded. When I got to the part about finding the ledger, he got excited.

"Where is it? Did you bring it with you?"

"It's in my purse." I pointed to the coatrack.

He jumped out of his chair and grabbed my bag, but instead of rooting around for the book, he handed it to me. I appreciated his respect for my privacy.

"Are your prints all over it?"

"Come on, you talk like I'm an amateur. No, I was very careful."

"I have some gloves here. Hold up a minute."

He went to a large filing cabinet by the door and pulled out a box of latex gloves. Then he took out two pairs and handed one to me before removing the book from the plastic bag.

I reluctantly took my feet off the chair so Nathan could sit. As we started reading through the entries together, neither one of us said a word. When we came to the last page, it was obvious we didn't understand what we'd just read.

"Do you recognize any of these names?" I asked. "You have to know at least one of these people."

"Look at those addresses: Paris, San Francisco, New York. I'm a hometown boy; how would I know these people?"

"I just hoped that between the two of us, something would click. Luckily we can Google anyone we want."

"Read off the spelling of the first guy," he said as he got behind his computer.

When I was finished rattling off the letters, we scrolled through the search results.

"Here it is. Says this guy is a movie executive and lives in Beverly Hills. His last three pictures grossed over a billion. Blah, blah . . . next project, a romance scheduled to be released in the winter . . . blah, blah . . . two children . . . married four times, divorced four times . . . here it is! The last wife tried to get half of his art collection, which is valued at one hundred million." Nathan whistled. "This dude's a serious collector."

We checked out the next three names in the ledger. The one thing all of them had in common, besides wealth, was their art collections.

"So Stacey was involved with these people somehow," I said. "The dollar amounts next to their name could mean a few things."

"Services rendered, commissions," Nathan said. "Or blackmail payments. Wow, this could be a whole new list of suspects."

"Or maybe she was just keeping the records for someone else who was doing one of those things."

"I'll keep the book here and run these names by Rosie tomorrow. That girl has a contact in every racketeering operation out there."

"Good." Then I told Nathan about my meeting with Cynthia Price at the bank.

"She sounds like a sad lady," Nathan said, after I finished.

"And so sweet. I think she wants this killer caught more than we do. She looked up records without one second of hesitation. Cynthia thought of Stacey more as a daughter than just a customer at the bank."

"Was there anything unusual in her checking account statements?"

"As a matter of fact, there was," I said. "Three

large amounts, electronically deposited from L'Etoile du Nord in New York. It's a charitable foundation that has funded schools and orphanages."

"So this book could just contain names of contributors along with the amount of their donations."

I shrugged. "Could be. But why would Stacey be keeping records for a huge organization in a little book hidden in her kitchen? Wouldn't they have accountants and lawyers for that?"

Nathan nodded.

"And don't you find it weird that the name of the foundation is French and that it's the state motto of Minnesota?"

"What if Stacey had money of her own and she's—"

"The girl was just scraping by. Her mother has cancer; there's thousands of dollars in medical bills and she owed credit card companies—she had to work two jobs just to make it."

"Okay, let's go with the obvious then," Nathan suggested. "The name is our state motto because it was either started by someone originally from Minnesota or someone who currently lives here. You know, for sentimental reasons. People do that all the time. They name a boat after a girlfriend or a racehorse after their favorite food."

"Or . . . it's called that because the person behind it is French. Like Antoine Rousseau. And there's something else. Mrs. Davidson's nurse told me that Antoine's a collector. When he gets wind of a painting he wants, he becomes obsessed. I bet that he took the job at the mansion because he'd heard about the Klimt."

"Wow." Nathan sat back to think a moment. "That makes perfect sense. So he meets Stacey who's desperate for money and, if we assume the ledger represents illegal activity, easily convinces her to help him find and then steal the painting."

"He'll add it to his collection and pay her for helping him."

"With some extra thrown in to keep her mouth shut," Nathan added.

"Wait a minute. I have a printout Cynthia gave me." I reached in my purse. Then I smoothed out the paper on top of Nathan's desk and pointed. "Three deposits from L'Etoile du Nord within the *last year*. But if they'd found the Klimt, that would account for only one deposit. And, according to what I heard, Stacey had only been working for Randolph for eight months. So what about the deposits before then?"

"Guess we've gone as far as we can for now. Let me show this to Rosie and we'll get back to you tomorrow."

"Great," I said and went to get my jacket. "I have to go home. I need a shower and a nice hot cup of tea. I'm pooped."

Nathan walked me to the front door. "I'll call you tomorrow."

Chapter Thirty~One

At two o'clock the next afternoon, I was in Dean Bostwick's office.

But he wasn't.

I figured he was still on some power trip, trying to show me who the real boss here was. But he forgot I had a lot more time than he did and a lot more patience. So I leaned back, sipped the cup of coffee I'd brought with me, and waited.

By 2:15, I'd finished my coffee.

A young officer walked by the open door then turned around to look in on me. "How're you doing, Mrs. Sullivan?"

"I'm fine."

"If there's anything you need, my name's Ben."

"Thanks, but I'm sure you have more important things to do than take care of me."

"Oh, it's no trouble. It's kinda slow around here today."

"That's a good thing . . . right?"

"Sure is." He smiled, then continued down the hall.

I decided to sit there all day if I had to. Luckily I'd tossed the latest issue of *Southwest Art* magazine in my tote bag before leaving home. I pulled it out and began reading about the La Quinta Art Festival.

Dean Bostwick came rushing in. "Have you been waiting long?"

I held up my right index finger. "Give me a minute. I'm almost done with this article."

He stood there, looking more confused than annoyed. Then he took off his suit jacket, draped it over the back of his desk chair, and sat quietly.

Score one for the retired lady police chief!

Slowly, I closed the magazine and put it back in my tote. I prolonged the simple task, enjoying being in control. Then I sat back. "So what do you have for me?"

Dean reached over to a pile of files on the right corner of his desk and removed the top one. "The coroner's report came in yesterday." He pushed it toward me.

I couldn't let on that I already knew what was in the report. So I picked up the file. As I read through it, I stopped every now and then, feigning interest.

Dean sat back, his hands clasped behind his head. "So what do you think?"

"I think it corroborates what I saw at the murder scene. Other than the part about metallic flakes being in the wound, there's not much new here."

"Any idea what the murder weapon could have been?"

"Are you asking for my opinion, Dean?"

"Look, I know I rode you pretty hard back then. You just took everything too personally. This is a young man's game, Katherine. Every day it's more crazy and dangerous out there. Cops are getting shot left and right."

He was right about it being a crazy world, but I didn't tell him so.

Then, as if trying to redeem himself, he said, "Did you know Stacey Jordan and Antoine Rousseau had worked together before? He hired her to evaluate a private art collection belonging to a family he was working for in Chicago."

"When was this?"

Bostwick picked up another file that had been underneath the coroner's report. Opening it, he flipped through two pages, then stopped. "From April to June of last year."

I reached for my note pad. "How do you know this?"

"Pierce's polygraph. He was asked how he first became acquainted with Stacey. He answered that she was recommended by Rousseau. He was then asked what exactly Rousseau had said about her. You know, ask the same question in a few different ways to try and trip him up."

"And did you?"

"Nope. Like I told you on the phone; he passed with flying colors. He met Stacey through

Rousseau. Since he was also opening an art gallery and there wasn't enough full-time work for her at the estate, he also had her fill in at the gallery."

"What exactly was she working on at the estate?"

"Cataloguing paintings, taking inventory of the various collections, things like that."

"And do you think there were other jobs before the one in Chicago?" I asked.

"Pierce didn't know of any. But she did work at a museum here in town for a while."

"The Miller Art Center."

He checked his file. "The Miller, yeah that's it."

I started to put my note pad back in my tote. "Well I have places to be, and even though it's a slow day around here, I'm sure you can find something to do." I couldn't leave without letting him know I was aware he'd kept me waiting for no good reason.

But he didn't acknowledge my remark. "So we're square now, right?"

"And you're not going to interfere with my investigation?"

"If you don't mess with mine . . . we're good," he said.

Chapter Thirty-Two

Lizzie was in front of the TV, arms folded in front of her. The redness of her eyes revealed she had been crying. "Where are the kids? Why are you home now? What's wrong?" I couldn't stop the questions from flying out of my mouth.

She looked up at me with those red eyes. "Daddy Dearest flew into town. He called telling me—not asking—that he'd be picking the kids up from school and keeping them overnight."

"When was this?"

"Around two."

I walked into the living room and sat next to her.

"I had to drop everything, come home, pack a bag for each of them, and take it to school. Then I had to ask Mr. Edstrom, the principal, to call them to his office so I could tell them what the heck was going on. Chloe doesn't have her phone . . . Not that I'm blaming any of this on you, Mother."

"Thank you. But doesn't Cam have a phone?"

"Half the time he leaves it at home—like he did today. And even if he had it and told Chloe, they'd still need a change of clothes."

"I thought they had clothes at Tom's."

She just looked at me, irritated that I was foisting logic on her while she was in such an emotional state. What she needed from me at that moment was a mother with a warm shoulder to cry on. So I wrapped my arms around her.

"It's just that poor Cammy," she whimpered, "he needs time to adjust to a new situation. Tom knows that. Their first night together is always difficult. Cam gets withdrawn and a little afraid. You can't just spring something unexpected on him."

"Aww, honey. Chloe will be with him and he's got a room at Tom's apartment. It's not as if he's been kidnapped by a stranger."

"I know." She put down a bag of cookies, picked up a tissue to wipe her eyes, and turned the TV off.

"So I get my daughter all to myself. How lucky am I?" I put on my happy face. "What'll we do? A movie? Shopping? Just name it. It's girl's night out."

She brightened up a little. "Really? You're not running out somewhere?"

"I'm all yours tonight."

And then, sheepishly, she said, "I know you don't want to hear this but I miss Randy. Things were going along great; I couldn't believe how much he'd changed. Then Stacey . . . I know I sound heartless but everything's all complicated now."

"Listen." I held her face between my hands. "If Randolph makes you happy, that's all I care about. And as for Tom, you know Cam loosens up after a few hours. By tonight, he won't want to come home."

Lizzie burst into tears. "That's what I'm afraid of."

"Stay there while I go get some paper," I told her.

She wiped her eyes again. "Paper? What are you talking about?"

"We have to make a list of all the things you need to start worrying about. We'll start with the car. What if you get a flat tire tomorrow? Or have an accident? Then we'll move on to the weather. What if it rains and you've left all the windows open?"

"You're being silly, Mother."

"No, sweetheart, you are. You have to learn to stop wasting time worrying about what-ifs."

After blowing her nose, Lizzie sat up straight. "I need a shower."

"Me, too."

"So let's get ready and meet back here in an hour."

"Sounds good," I said, brushing a curl off her forehead.

We ended up at the Galleria. To atone for all the fattening foods we'd been eating, dinner was at an organic café. Then shopping. Neither one of us really needed anything except to spend time together, and browsing through beautiful stores had always been one of our favorite indoor sports.

We talked over sale racks, gawked through windows of stores neither one of us could afford to shop in, and tried on shoes. Lizzie bought a few summer things for herself and the kids. I picked up the latest celebrity biography and a scarf. When we were finally too tired to even ride the escalator, we sat down in the food court to people watch and enjoy a cool drink.

"I went to see your illustrious chief of police today," I said after arranging my packages on the vacant seat next to me.

Lizzie held up her smoothie. "Since we're talking business, I guess this is deductible."

"I never thought of it that way, but you're right. What about my new scarf? If I wear it while I'm here—"

"Don't push it, Mother." She laughed. "So what did dear Mr. Bostwick have to say?"

"He told me you and Randolph took the polygraph and passed with flying colors. His exact words—flying colors."

"So when will Randy get out?" she asked anxiously. "Did he say?"

"Oh, he's still playing hardball, but it'll be soon. Within the next few days, I'd guess."

Lizzie looked relieved. "Is that all you and Dean talked about?"

"We also discussed Antoine Rousseau."

"How did his name come up?" she asked.

"Apparently, during the lie detector test, Randolph was asked who had referred Stacey for the job at the estate. He said that Antoine had. Did you know that?"

Lizzie stopped to think a moment. "I vaguely remember him telling me she'd come highly recommended, that's all."

"I guess he was trying to distance himself from her as much as possible."

"And he's afraid of saying anything that'll incriminate him," Lizzie added.

Then I told her all about my trip to Minneapolis and going to Stacey's house. I glossed over the part about how I got inside and she didn't ask any questions; she just sat, listening intently. It was too soon to mention the ledger, so I didn't. If Rosie couldn't come up with some more evidence linked to it, it was still just a book. I did tell her, however, about meeting with Cynthia Price and the questionable deposits to Stacey's account.

"Then Bostwick told me he'd found evidence that Antoine and Stacey had worked together before, maybe several times, on jobs involving private art collections."

Lizzie's eyes got big. "Are you thinking that maybe he killed her?"

"It's a possibility. Nathan's checking out some things for me. I'll know more tomorrow."

"So you saw Nathan, too?"

I nodded. "Just before I came home."

"And it was just a business call?"

"Yes," I said. "Why the grin? What else would I go to his office for?"

"It's obvious he likes you, Mother," Lizzie kidded. "So what do you think about him? It's okay, you know. Daddy's been gone awhile and you're still so pretty and vibrant . . ."

Our night together was turning out like I'd hoped it would. We were sitting there, kidding each other, laughing. The mood was light and I tried keeping it that way when I told her, "We live in different places and both of us have a lot of baggage . . ."

"But you've thought about it, haven't you?" she giggled. "Maybe just a few times?"

I could feel my face warming up. "Maybe." She was enjoying making me squirm.

"And if that doesn't work out," she smiled, "there's always Tinder."

I stirred the fruit around in my drink. "What's that? Sounds like a lumberjack camp."

"No, it's a dating site for mature singles. You can go online, sign up, and meet men in your area."

"You sound like a commercial."

"I'm serious, Mother. I don't like to think of you being all alone."

"Do I look like I'm lonely? Like I need a man?"

"No."

I patted her hand. "I'm fine . . . really."

"Okay, I believe you."

"Good. Now I'm dead on my feet and want to go home."

We gathered up our packages and headed for the parking lot. But we had to pass my favorite jewelry store on the way. And of course, I had to have a look inside.

The diamonds sparkled brilliantly beneath fluorescent lights. Earrings and bracelets were arranged on top of the blue velvet lining inside display cases. "Oh, I forgot to tell you," Lizzie suddenly said, pointing to a jeweled cuff. "I saw Jackie Pierce today. She was wearing something similar to that. She looked as strange as ever."

"Where was this?" I asked, putting down the gold earrings I'd been admiring.

"At the bank. I ran in to use the ATM and there she was talking to Mr. Branson."

"Owen? I haven't seen him in years."

"Well, he's the manager now."

"Was she alone?"

"Do you mean was that big lunkhead with her?"

"I don't think he's such a lunkhead. Maybe he has us all fooled."

"No—at least I didn't see him. It was just Jackie in all her glory."

"And did you talk to her?" I asked.

Lizzie looked so proud of herself when she said, "I did one better. I waited around until she was gone and then went in to see Mr. Branson."

I grilled her all the way to the car. While we put our packages in the trunk, I questioned her some more. On the ride home, we were still talking about Jacqueline Pierce.

"She was making inquiries about the family estate. Mr. Branson said she's been in and out of his office for days."

"You told me you saw her around town before I got here. That first time I went to see Randolph in prison, she made a scene and told the officer she'd just flown in from Las Vegas. She gave the impression that she'd come specifically to help her poor nephew."

"Mr. Branson said she told him she was living out at the guesthouse. Jackie said she had permision to be there. Just because Randy's grandfather and father didn't want her on the property, that doesn't mean he feels the same way," Lizzie told me.

"So she's been out there the whole time? Even before Stacey was murdered? Randolph had to have known."

"He knew she used it when she came to visit, which wasn't very often. Randy and his aunt have always been polite to each other. She's really the only family he has left. And he feels sorry for her."

"It's easy to tolerate anyone for a few days," I said.

"But he did tell me that as the centennial gets closer and Buckhorn's almost ready to be turned over to the state, she's more agitated and won't stop calling him. Night and day, she gets all worked up, threatening, shouting that the mansion's hers."

"Wasn't he concerned?" I asked.

"No. He just thinks Jackie's crazy and hasn't got the money or brains to organize any kind of legal plan."

"What about her . . . friend?"

"Hank?" Lizzie laughed. "He's got an IQ of ten. The guy's an idiot."

Chapter Thirty-Three

Lizzie called the kids when we got home. She made plans to pick them up after school the next day. I got in my hellos and good-byes. They seemed happy to be with their father.

I rummaged through my tote bag and finally found the note pad I'd been using during the investigation. Then I sat at the kitchen table to organize my thoughts. Flipping through the pages, I reviewed everything I'd learned over the course of my investigation. When I was finished, I made a list of what I planned to do the next day. At the very top was *Go out to Buckhorn—talk to Jackie Pierce.*

I looked at the clock by my bed; it was eight. Throwing on my robe, I walked out to see what my daughter was up to.

Lizzie sat perched on a high stool in front of the marble counter. She looked very professional in a gray suit. She wore pants so often that I wasn't used to seeing her legs. Those black suede heels of hers were perfect.

"Wow," I stopped to admire her, "talk about dressed for success. You nailed it, kiddo."

She looked up from the laptop propped open

on the counter in front of her. "Thanks. I have to be in court at ten." She got up. "Want some coffee?"

"Always." I sat on the stool next to hers.

"What's the case?"

"I'm helping a woman get her child support increased. It's gotten real messy between her and the father."

Lizzie refilled her cup and then brought it back to the counter along with one for me.

"Sometimes I forget you're all grown up, a respected member of the community. When I'm out in Taos I think of you as just . . . Lizzie. My little girl. And then I come back here and BAM! There's this beautiful grown woman, with two children of her own, running an office, and it kind of rattles me. It takes a few minutes to take it all in."

Lizzie grinned. "Welcome to my world." She sat down. "Now you know how I felt."

"What do you mean?"

"You were my loving mother, the one who made cookies and colored with me. Daddy and I were the only people you took care of. Then I'd go to the station and you were wearing a uniform, not T-shirts and jeans like at home. Policemen were reporting to you; you had a big office. And you weren't the same mother I had at home. You were the freakin' chief of police! I realized then that when you left home, you were taking care of hundreds of strangers. I got a little jealous sometimes."

I reached out and stroked her hair. "Well now I'm just a wandering artist."

Lizzie rolled her eyes. "Come on, Mother, you've never been 'just' anything."

"Neither have you, my dear."

"Here's to the Sullivan women," Lizzie said, raising her coffee cup. And we toasted each other.

We talked for a few minutes more before she left the house. When I was alone, I called Nathan.

"Has Rosie come in yet?" I asked him.

"She'll be here any minute. I told her all about Stacey's book, and she plans to work on it all day. What's on your schedule?"

"I'm going out to Buckhorn to talk to Jackie Pierce."

"Why?"

"Last night Lizzie told me that Jackie's trying to get documentation stating the mansion belongs to her."

"And you think her legal problems had something to do with how she felt about Stacey?"

"I think they might have contributed to her state of mind."

"Oh, that woman's always been a little psycho."

"Sometimes I think her craziness is all an act just so she can keep getting away with things. People don't really see or take time to listen to a crazy person. They'll do whatever they can to just make them go away. I think she's counting on the police to do the same."

Nathan took a deep breath. "I'm not going to try and talk you out of this but I—"

"You insist on coming with me, right?"

"Now don't get mad, Kathy but—"

"I want you to come this time, Nathan. That's why I called."

"Well, I'm glad to hear that you've come to your senses."

Chapter Thirty-Four

Nathan picked me up at the house an hour later.

"So how do you plan on handling this?" he asked after we'd pulled out of the driveway.

"I'll be friendly but direct. I'm not going to let her distract me with accusations or insults. Once we're inside, I'll calmly ask her a few questions."

"Sure, that would be great. But you can't be sure what we're going to find out there," he said.

"What do you mean?"

"A kook like her could have a dozen cats or garbage piled up to the ceiling. You never know."

"I think we can handle small animals or garbage." I settled back in my seat.

"What if she sics that big guy of hers on us?"

"Hank? He spends all his time at the gym; he probably won't even be there."

"Well just in case . . ." Nathan patted the shoulder holster concealed beneath his jacket.

What the Pierce family referred to as a guesthouse would have been more than adequate for a family of four. It was a bungalow, built in the same style as the mansion. But while the estate had been made of brick and stained glass, the small house had been constructed of wood, featuring beveled windows. A thick grove of trees surrounded it, creating a forest setting. Heavy drapes covered the windows.

We didn't speak as we approached.

An Adirondack chair had been dragged out to the front of the house. Grooves in the dirt around the patio told me it had to have been moved by Jackie. Hank would have just picked it up, so logically it followed that Jackie was living there alone.

As we got closer, I could hear voices inside. "Someone's in there," I whispered to Nathan.

He nodded.

I walked to the door and knocked. Nathan stood behind me, covering my back.

The voices stopped.

Nathan and I waited, but no one came.

I knocked again. "Jackie? This is Katherine Sullivan and Nathan Walker. We want to talk to you."

Still no response.

Then I pounded on the door with my fist. "I'm trying to prove that your nephew didn't kill Stacey Jordan. Don't you want to help me get him out of jail?" Maybe that would get her attention.

The door opened a crack.

Jackie's wrinkled face looked up at me. "Mrs. Sullivan. My, my, you certainly are persistent, aren't you? Just like an old dog hanging onto his favorite bone for dear life."

"Do you think you can put aside your dislike for me just long enough to answer a few questions? I know we both want to clear Randolph of this murder charge."

She opened the door slightly wider and I could see Hank inside. "My nephew's the only reason I came back to this godforsaken town. I'd do anything for that darling boy. How dare you act as though you and Elizabeth are the only people who care about his welfare."

Nathan stepped forward. "We just need a few minutes and then we'll get out of your hair. Being difficult will only make this drag on longer than it has to."

"The guy makes sense, babe," Hank said. "Let 'em in so we can get this the hell over with."

Grudgingly, Jackie opened the door completely. Turning her back on us, she walked into the house and we followed.

The floor in the entryway was gray granite. To the right was a black wooden bench, next to that an umbrella stand. To the left, in the middle of the wall, was a small table. It had also been painted black, and on top of it was a 1950s-style phone, which probably had been put there more for its style than function.

A large fireplace took up the bottom half of a back wall in the main room; embers glowed around a single log. Along the wide mantle were clusters of photographs in gold and silver frames, sharing space with a collection of glass vases. The floor and baseboards had been made from rich dark wood. Above the mantle was a large oil painting of purple and white wildflowers in a field of green. An oversized couch covered in red and navy tapestry was turned toward the fireplace. Someone was sitting on it, and I could see the back of a head as we walked further into the room. When he heard us, he stood up. I don't know why, but I was surprised to see Antoine Rousseau . . . again.

"Mrs. Sullivan, what an unexpected pleasure." Then, looking at Nathan, he held out his hand. "I don't believe I've had the honor; I am Antoine Rousseau."

While the men shook hands, I said, "This is Officer Nathan Walker. We worked together on the force; he was my husband's partner." I was hoping by throwing in an official title that maybe Nathan would command more respect than I had been getting. I also wanted to intimidate Rousseau.

Turning to Nathan, I said, "You remember me talking about Mr. Rousseau, don't you? He's an art conservationist. He was hired by the board of directors at Buckhorn to oversee the restoration."

"Sure, I remember," he told me. Then to Rousseau he said, "I've heard a lot about you from Mrs. Sullivan and Mr. Pierce as well."

It obviously pleased the Frenchman knowing that he had been the main topic of several conversations. Smiling, he nodded smugly and straightened his tie.

Watching him, I realized I had never seen Antoine dressed casually. He wore a business suit like a coat of armor, making him always seem guarded, prepared for any occasion. That day was no exception. His brown suit was perfectly pressed; every single button of the taupe shirt beneath was fastened. His tie was chocolate brown and taupe plaid. Sticking out of a breast pocket was a handkerchief that matched the tie. When he moved his hands, expensive-looking gold cuff links glimmered. His highly polished shoes reflected the light from a Tiffany lamp on a small table near the window.

"And I, you." Antoine said, then looked perplexed as to what to do next.

"I'm glad to find you here, too, Mr. Rousseau, I've got a few questions for you as well."

"I told you everything I could that day at my hotel."

"Well, during my investigation, I've come up with some more questions."

Even Hank was dressed more formally. He'd put on his big-boy pants that day: clean khakis with a sharp crease running down the front of each leg. A pale yellow polo shirt sporting a designer logo made his tan pop. But he still couldn't bring himself to buy the correct size. This one was a few sizes too small, making his bulging biceps look like a mountain range beneath the fabric.

Jackie slowly walked toward a chair by the fireplace. It was strange that I'd never noticed she had a slight limp. As she passed by me, her sweet, floral perfume polluted the air. She scuffed her shoes—black satin ballet slippers—across the Persian rug. The hem of each leg of her white jumpsuit dragged along the floor, collecting dust as she walked. A purple cardigan trimmed with pink ribbon flowers hung around her shoulders.

"Sit!" Jackie barked and pointed to a love seat covered in the same tapestry as the couch.

As I came around the sofa, I could see a mahogany table in front of it. Three wine glasses were spread across its surface. Two of the glasses were half full of a ruby liquid; one was empty. A bottle of Merlot sat in the middle. It was too early in the day to start drinking, which meant the glasses and wine were still there from the night before or the three of them had been celebrating something when we interrupted.

While I walked to a seat, I calculated my next move. Who should I question first? But Jackie took charge and eliminated any further planning on my part.

"Before we begin, I want to make it clear that it

is only because of my concern for my nephew that I've let you in my home. And believe me, this is indeed my home. The authorities have granted me access. You, on the other hand, are trespassing on private property. And if Mr. Walker is indeed an officer of the law," she cocked an eyebrow at Nathan, "I could have him arrest you whenever it pleases me."

Nathan started to reach for his wallet to produce his official, expired police ID, but she waved him off.

"From what I've learned during my investigation, none of you has any right being here." I glanced around the room at the three of them. "But why quibble over technicalities?"

Jackie stuck out her jaw, looking at me with disdain.

"My sources tell me that Stacey Jordan was getting a little too . . . nosey? Is that the right word, Mr. Rousseau?" I turned toward Antoine. "Was she getting in your way?"

The man looked shocked. "Are you trying to say that maybe I would have harmed that beautiful girl?"

"You were with her that day—her last day at the mansion."

"Why the very thought . . . that I could ever . . . this is preposterous!"

Hank came over and sat on the arm of Jackie's chair. He started to laugh. "If you think Frenchie over there has the guts to kill someone, think again," he said to me.

Antoine looked insulted at first but then joined in the laughing, realizing Hank had just handed him an excuse. "Oui, it is true. I work with my brain, not my muscles. Physical labor is for uneducated men." He shot a look back at Hank who seemed to take the remark as a compliment.

But could Slater really be that dumb? Or was it an act?

I continued. "And my sources tell me that you've had several run-ins with the law, Mr. Slater."

"I know all about Hank's . . . indiscretions, Mrs. Sullivan. If you're trying to shock me, you'll have to try harder," Jackie grumbled.

"Okay, how about this?" I asked. "Would you be shocked to learn that your father's stories about there being a Klimt hidden in Buckhorn were true? And that the painting has been found?" I never flinched, waiting for her reaction to my bluff.

Jackie's fingers worked nervously, twisting a too large bracelet around her bony wrist. "And where exactly is the painting now?"

"In a safe place. With the authorities."

Hank started to say something but Jackie squeezed his knee, signaling him to shut up.

Antoine picked up one of the wineglasses and emptied it in two gulps. The four of us watched in silence as he wiped the bottom of the goblet with a napkin before setting it back on the table.

Watching him fuss that way, I suddenly believed Hank. This fastidious man could never stain his hands with a victim's blood. Murder always involved some degree of passion, which he seemed to lack altogether. No, Antoine Rousseau was an instigator, a calculating planner, not a murderer.

"So, in your esteemed opinion, the only reason someone would have to murder Miss Jordan was to steal the painting from her," Jackie said in a matter-of-fact way. "But if the police have the Klimt now, they must have tracked down the killer to get it. And since none of us have set eyes on it—"

"—I certainly have not," Antoine said.

Hank smiled. "Me neither."

"Then I don't understand why you and Mr. Walker are here at all."

She thought she had me with her lopsided logic. I nodded, hoping that if I stayed quiet, she'd take the chance to gloat a little more and incriminate herself or her friends.

"And if that poor girl was still alive, I'm sure she would have sold the painting as soon as possible. Because she needed money desperately," Jackie said.

And there it was. I grabbed the clue and ran with it.

"How do you know anything about Stacey's financial affairs?" I asked.

"Well . . . I could tell from the way she dressed. You know, breeding shows in everything about a person." She stuck her nose in the air. "Besides, why on earth would she be working at Buckhorn as well as at Randolph's gallery if it wasn't for the money?"

"Maybe she was having it off with her boss?" Hank laughed. "It wouldn't be the first time a girl tried to sleep her way to the top."

I could feel my jaw clenching. "And just where would the top be in this situation, Mr. Slater?"

"Come on, you know what I mean. Don't act insulted. We're all adults here."

I'd promised myself I wouldn't let Jackie get to me, and now it was Hank who was pushing my buttons. Nathan caught my eye, shooting me a look that warned me to calm down.

"Is there anything else?" Jackie asked.

"Oh yes, we're far from done here," I said.

"You're trying my patience, Mrs. Sullivan."

"Yeah, we don't have all day, ya know," Hank complained.

Ignoring both of them, I continued. "I'm having trouble with your logic. Why would you assume that finding the painting means also finding the killer? The police could have located the Klimt while investigating the murder scene, after

Stacey had been killed and was found—alone—at the mansion."

"I never claimed to be a private investigator. I believe that's your job. And it seems to me that you're just grabbing at straws. You came here looking for someone else to blame Miss Jordan's death on instead of examining the facts.

"Okay, here's a fact, Ms. Pierce. You arrived in Edina *before* Stacey was killed, correct?"

"No, I came afterwards, when Randolph was arrested." I didn't bother correcting her.

"Funny, I know for a fact you were in town several days before. Owen Branson, the manager at First National, said that you'd been in to see him about a legal matter."

"He has his dates wrong, that's all."

"Well, there aren't that many flights from Las Vegas each day. I can always check with the airlines."

"What does any of this matter?" Jackie asked. "None of us in this room killed Stacey Jordan. Why on earth would we?"

"Let's suppose she found the Klimt and wouldn't give it to you," Nathan said.

"Now you're just inventing a story, Mr. Walker. I think we're finished here."

The more agitated she became, the calmer I got. "I'm sure Chief Bostwick has warned you not to leave town?"

"Yes," she said. The only color on her face were her flushed cheeks.

"Okay then." I turned away from her. "Mr. Rousseau, I mentioned finding out some new information. If you'd be so kind to indulge me?"

"But of course."

I took my time getting the note pad out of my bag. Tension hovered over the room like a storm cloud. "Was this the first time you worked with Stacey Jordan? During the renovation at Buckhorn?"

Rousseau looked at Jackie, uncertain how to answer. When she didn't say anything, he answered, "No . . . not exactly."

I flipped through my notes. "If my sources are correct, you worked with her last year in Chicago, at a similar job." There—I'd laid it out for him and he knew he couldn't lie about his past associations with Stacey.

As if suddenly remembering, he said, "Yes, I must have forgotten."

"And how did you happen to be working with her again?"

"Oh . . ." He brushed off his pant leg even though there wasn't anything to brush off. "Let me see . . . I was hired to work here and asked if I could recommend someone to assist me. Mademoiselle Jordan was just one of many I mentioned. So I guess it was a coincidence."

Nathan snickered. "There's no such thing as

a coincidence, Mr. Rousseau. At least not in a police investigation."

"Well, in life there certainly is." Antoine smiled at him.

I pretended to be confused. "I can certainly understand if that last job slipped your mind. You are a busy man and your job takes you all over the world."

"This is true."

"But you've worked with Stacey on at least three other occasions. In fact, over the past few years you, personally, have made several large deposits to her account here in Edina." I looked up, waiting for his reaction.

"My accountant handles such things through my foundation."

I couldn't believe my luck and decided to go for broke. "So L'Etoile du Nord was set up by you?"

"Oui."

"Why would a French citizen, living in Paris, name a foundation after the state motto of Minnesota?" Nathan asked. "Another coincidence, Mr. Rousseau?"

"In a way . . . I guess. My accountant is American . . ." He seemed to be making his story up as he went along. And he wasn't doing a very good job of it.

"Well what are the chances of that happening?" I asked.

Antoine shrugged. "'Tis a very small world indeed."

I checked my notes again, just for show, and looked up as if I'd suddenly remembered something. "Oh, did I mention that among Miss Jordan's belongings was a book with a list of names? My office is going through it now. I think it may be people you worked for on other projects as well. The dollar amount next to their names must have to do with expenses or something like that?" I looked at him quizzically. "Do you have any idea what that might be about?"

There it was, at last. His cool veneer was slipping, and he looked startled and a little alarmed.

"I would have to see this book before commenting."

"I understand." Then, looking at Nathan, I asked, "Is there anything you'd like to ask?"

"Yes." He glared at Hank.

"A few nights ago we were on the grounds and were accosted by three men."

"Are you accusing me of somethin'?" Hank asked. "'Cause if you are . . ." He jumped up, coming at Nathan.

"Sit down!" Jackie shouted.

Like an obedient pet, Hank sat back down next to his mistress.

"Now, Mr. Walker, as I've told you before, this

264

is private property. You had no right being here, especially in the dead of night. And may I ask why you were here to begin with?"

"Searching for the murder weapon," he lied without hesitation.

Jackie looked at him, scrutinizing his face. "Now we're done here."

I stood up, eager to be out of there. "Thank you all for your cooperation."

Jackie led the way to the door. As she reached out to grab the knob, her bracelet fell to the floor. Hank bent down to pick it up.

"What a beautiful piece," I said. "I remember admiring it that day in front of the gallery."

Her face twisted up into a smile. She rubbed Hank's arm. "It's a present from my teddy bear."

"Wherever did you buy it?" I asked Hank. "My daughter's birthday is coming up and I'd love to get her—"

"Can't remember," he said and put the bracelet back on Jackie's wrist, kissing her hand. "But nothing's too good for my girl."

Chapter Thirty-Five

"All that 'babe' and 'teddy bear' talk made it really hard to take those two seriously." Nathan said as we walked to his car.

"Jackie sure seemed to be eating up the attention."

"Why wouldn't she?" he asked. "A younger, handsome man—he is handsome, right?"

"Most women would think so."

"Okay. A younger, handsome man fussing over her like that. Buying her expensive jewelry."

"He didn't buy that bracelet," I said, getting into the car. "I remember seeing one like it on Stacey's wrist at the gallery. He could have stolen it from Stacey while she was alive—"

"—or took it from her after she was dead. But can you prove it's the same one?" Nathan asked as he turned on the ignition.

"It's a memorable piece. I'm sure I can get statements from people who saw her wearing it. Or maybe there's a receipt in her house. But I'd have to examine it first. Maybe there's something engraved inside . . . something that will help identify it as belonging to her."

"Good luck prying it off Jackie's wrist."

"That shouldn't be too difficult. You saw how

it just fell off. And did you notice that umbrella stand just inside the door?" I asked.

"Not really."

"Besides umbrellas, there were a few canes. One had a metal knob on top. I've seen it before. It's Antoine's."

Nathan turned. "Want me to go back and grab it? Then you can take it to Barb."

"No. We don't want to tip our hand. And . . . I might be wrong. Besides, it has to be taken officially, or it's inadmissible."

"You should know, Chief," he said, with a wink. "But first we have to stop at the office. I want to see how Rosie's coming along with that ledger."

As we drove, Nathan and I talked about what had just happened in the guesthouse. We agreed that if Antoine, Jackie, or Hank had been involved in the murder that Antoine was most likely the mastermind behind it.

"But there's always the chance that a worker, some stranger, who had been on the property everyday heard the rumors and happened to walk in when Stacey found the painting. They struggled. When she wouldn't give it up, he killed her," Nathan said, playing devil's advocate.

"It's possible," I agreed. "But if that was the case, she couldn't have been struck from behind.

Unless . . . there were two people there that night."

"True," Nathan said, staring at the road ahead.

"But you and I both know that ninety-nine point nine percent of all murders are committed by someone the victim knew."

"What if Stacey had been dating one of the construction guys? She told him, in an intimate moment, about finding the painting and . . . it even sounds farfetched to me as I'm saying it," Nathan admitted. "No, if we take Randolph out of the mix, it had to be one of those characters back there."

"So you haven't completely eliminated Randolph, have you?"

"Sorry. I know he's involved with Lizzie and all but . . ."

"That has no bearing on the case," I said. "Go on."

"Well, talk about motive. The guy's handing over his family's estate, losing all claim to it. He's been raised on stories of valuable artwork hidden in the walls. What a perfect smokescreen. Claiming that the renovations are to get the house ready for the centennial while all the time he's really searching for paintings—anything of value. Then when some-thing's found, the workmen plaster over the wall and Randolph, who has friends on the art scene in New York, puts feelers out to find a buyer."

"And if he did find a buyer or word on the street was that he was looking, wouldn't Rosie know about it? Or at least be able to find someone who does?" I asked.

"Positively."

Her Harley was parked in front of Nathan's office. I was eager to see how far she'd gotten deciphering the ledger and hurried into the building.

A radio was blaring good old rock and roll. Rosie didn't hear us come in and was sitting with her back to the door, hunched over Stacey's ledger. At the top of her lungs, she sang along with the music. Amused, Nathan and I waited until the song was over and then started to applaud. Startled, Rosie spun around in her chair.

When she saw it was us, she stood up and took a bow. "Thank you, thank you, I'll be signing autographs later."

"You sounded good," I told her.

"Yeah, well next time cough or something. Will ya?"

Nathan walked over to an empty desk and grabbed the chair in front of it, rolling it next to Rosie's. I did the same and sat on the other side of her.

"So what do you make of it?" he asked her, nodding toward the ledger, which was open on the desk next to her computer.

"After making a few calls, sending some e-mails, I can account for each and every name in there." Rosie sat back, resting her folded hands on her stomach.

I couldn't believe it had been so easy. "You mean you're done? You know what all those names and numbers mean?"

"Yep." She looked so proud of herself. "That's what I mean."

"Then tell us," Nathan said.

"Each name is a private collector. A very rich, powerful private collector who will do any-thing—and I mean anything—to get what they want. With these people, it's all about having what no one else has." She picked up the book and turned a page, then pointed to the name in the middle. "Like this guy. He collects Peruvian artifacts. He's paid a fortune to have pieces smuggled out of the country. He has pottery found at an archeological site that was on its way to a museum." She turned another page. "And this woman is using an old bomb shelter to hide and protect her Egyptian gold pieces."

"What about the dollar amounts recorded next to their name?" I asked.

"It's what they paid just for one particular item."

"And if the authorities had this book, would they all be arrested?" Nathan asked.

"And their collections confiscated," Rosie said.

"Did you talk to any of these people?" I asked.

"Oh God, no. None of them would even pick up the phone for a nobody like me."

"Not even if they thought you might have information to blackmail them with?"

"If they knew this book existed . . . let's just say any one of them would kill to get it."

I thought a moment and then asked, "So how does Stacey figure into all this?"

"You're gonna love this," Rosie said. "She was the go-between. Your fancy Mr. Rousseau made the initial contact when he worked on a house or at a museum. That's how he met Stacey, at a museum party. When he figured out she needed cash, and lots of it, he paid her to steal a painting or whatnot. Then he'd pay her more to shut up and sell the piece for ten times what he gave her. This book represents jobs she's done for Frenchie."

"Your sources knew Antoine?" I couldn't believe it. "They said his name? Described him? There's no mistake?"

"None. It's him all right."

I fell back in my chair. Nathan sat staring at the ledger.

"You know what we have to do, don't you?" he asked.

"Push Antoine until he cracks," I said.

"Like a walnut." Rosie said and laughed. "Like a big ol' walnut."

"But how do we . . . ?" I didn't get to finish asking my question when my cell phone rang. I didn't recognize the number. "Hello?"

"Mrs. Sullivan?"

"Yes."

"This is Antoine Rousseau."

I motioned to Nathan and Rosie that Antoine was on the other end.

"Yes, Mr. Rousseau?"

"I must see you. As soon as possible. Please come to the inn. You remember the place?"

"Yes."

"When can you be here?"

"In about an hour—hour and a half."

"Good. And Mrs. Sullivan?"

"Yes?"

"Please don't bring anyone with you."

After hanging up, I said, "Well, Nathan, you'll be surprised to know that coincidences really do happen."

"What did Rousseau want?"

"He wants me to come to his hotel right away."

Nathan started to get up.

"You're staying here," I told him. "He wants me to come alone."

"No way!"

Rosie grabbed Nathan's arm. "Relax, Boss. Aren't you the one goin' on all the time about how this lady can handle herself? And it's just a meeting. You can drive along—"

"That won't work," I told them. "Have you been out to the inn?"

They both nodded.

"Then you know you can't see into the rooms like you can at a motel. It's a huge building, four or five stories high, with a big lobby and two banks of elevators. There's no way you'd be able to know what's going on inside."

"You're just putting yourself in danger," he said. "Come on, Kathy, it could be a trap."

"I'm well aware of that."

He started to offer up another argument but I wouldn't let him.

"Nathan, aren't you the one who always tells me that I have good instincts? That I should trust my gut feelings?"

"Well . . ."

"Trust me, I can handle Antoine Rousseau."

When he finally realized he couldn't change my mind, he told me to at least take his .22, which he kept in the office. Just in case.

I agreed.

Chapter Thirty-Six

Lights around Lake Minnetonka were starting to come on as I parked in front of the inn. I'd listened to talk radio during the drive, not really paying attention to the subject matter, while I plotted my next few moves. But I did catch the weather report. That night there was supposed to be a full moon. More arrests were usually reported during a full moon. It wasn't just an old wives' tale that the world suddenly seemed to be overpopulated with lunatics on those nights. I just hoped that Antoine Rousseau wasn't one of the crazies.

He'd given me his room number, so there was no need to stop at the front desk this time. I walked straight through the lobby and to the bank of elevators located in the middle of the building. As I stood waiting, I looked down in my bag to make sure Nathan's gun was within reach. Maybe I'd been foolish mentioning Stacey's ledger earlier at the guesthouse, but there didn't seem to be any point in making this investigation drag on longer than it had to. And my strategy must have worked out because I'd gotten an immediate reaction from Antoine.

But letting him know about the book might have pushed him into a corner too soon. How far was he willing to go to protect his reputation and bank accounts? If somehow he'd found out that Stacey was keeping records of their transactions while she was alive, would he have been desperate enough to kill her?

The elevator doors finally opened. The car was empty and I stepped inside. There was a security camera in one corner, near the ceiling. Aware that sort of security system was never equipped with sound, I pulled out my driver's license and held it up. Then I flashed four fingers, then two, then three, signifying Antoine's room number: four twenty-three. Maybe it was silly. There had been many times—too many to count—when I was on the force and called to the scene of a burglary. The victims proudly pointed to their elaborate security system. But when they tried showing us the video, there was none because they'd failed to turn the darn thing on. Well at least I'd tried leaving evidence that I'd been there and where I was headed.

I knocked once and was raising my hand to follow it with another when the door jerked open. Antoine stood there, perspiration beaded along his forehead.

"Come in," he told me. "Hurry."

After I was inside the room, he walked out into the hallway and checked in both directions. When he was satisfied no one had followed me, he closed the door. His hands were shaking as he secured the chain then turned the deadbolt.

"I don't mean to be so mysterious but I fear I am being followed. Please, sit down."

The room was larger than the one he'd stayed in last time—not a full suite but what was referred to as a minisuite. There was one large room with a bed on one end and a couch, television set, and desk on the other.

"Are you all right, Mr. Rousseau? You look ill." I sat in a chair by the window, putting my tote bag on the floor, keeping it close to me.

"I haven't been right since coming to this horrible place."

"And why is that?"

Antoine sat down. He was still wearing the same clothes he'd had on earlier. But the way he was perspiring made his suit look confining, as if it was shrinking. I took off my jacket; just looking at him made me uncomfortable.

"You are a very smart woman, Mrs. Sullivan. You must know by now what Miss Jordan was up to." He waited for me to fill in the blanks.

But I just nodded, needing more information before I spoke.

"I first made her acquaintance three years ago when I was working as the head consultant on a project in Milwaukee. It was a large estate belonging to a very prominent family. The building was to be used for hospice care patients. When the project was complete, there was a cocktail party. My staff was invited, as well as doctors, patients, and their families. There were hundreds in attendance that night."

"And that's where you met Stacey?"

"Yes. Of course, I first reacted to her beauty. How could I not? She was breathtaking. As we talked, she told me about her mother, so distressed over the mounting medical bills. When I asked about her background, we found out we had our great appreciation and love of art in common.

"After a few dinners, and many drinks, I came to respect her intelligence. She was an educated, charming woman." He stopped a moment remembering happier times. "It was on one of those occasions that she told me of finding a rare statue in the attic of an elderly woman she worked for part time. Out of desperation to help her mother, she asked if I knew of someone who would pay for the piece."

"And you helped her?"

"Not at first. I am very respected in my field, Mrs. Sullivan, I couldn't take the chance—"

"Look, Mr. Rousseau, I'm just trying to find out who killed Ms. Jordan. I'm not interested in art theft or fraud. That's for a whole different set of police. So have no fear that I am going to call the FBI or Interpol."

He looked somewhat relieved.

"So why don't you just cut to the chase and

tell me what happened when you came to Edina?"

"Bon. But first I must have a drink; my nerves are shattered. Would you like something?"

"Thank you that would be nice." I was worried Antoine would pass out before he could finish his story and decided to slow down and take my time with him.

"I'll call down for some wine. Do you have a particular preference?"

"No. Whatever you decide is good."

He picked up the phone and called room service.

"It will take several minutes." He was ever the polite host, even in what was obviously a most difficult time for him.

"While we wait, could you please continue?" I suggested. "You were telling me about coming to town."

Antoine sat back down and loosened his tie. "I was contacted by a board member representing the Pierce estate. I was asked to fly in to oversee the renovations."

Gently, I said, "Yes, I know, we've been over this before, Mr. Rousseau."

"Forgive me." He smiled weakly. "I contacted Miss Jordan, remembering she was from this part of the country. It was then that she told me the rumors about Marshall Pierce smuggling stolen art out of Europe during the war. It was said he had them hidden in the walls of his mansion."

I smiled. "I grew up hearing those stories. But I never thought they were true."

"Believe me, Mrs. Sullivan, there are great treasures hidden in the strangest of places."

"So you believed Stacey when she talked about the Klimt?"

"Most definitely. That is why I persuaded the board to hire her as my assistant. Stacey and I agreed that it would be the perfect opportunity to allow us to search the mansion thoroughly."

"Was it you who found something?"

"No. Miss Jordan did."

"And you saw it? With your own eyes?" My heart was racing; I wanted to hear every detail.

"Oui. It was magnificent. A Klimt in perfect condition. A miracle, really, considering what it had been through."

"So where is it now?"

"I would assume you knew. After all, you told us that the authorities have it." Antoine smiled slyly. "But of course, my dear Mrs. Sullivan, we knew—you and I—that the other one was . . . how you say . . . fibbing?"

"You caught me, Mr. Rousseau. I fell back on my tried and true interrogation methods. So tell me please, where is the painting and did you find more than one piece?"

"Only the one, I'm afraid. And it is hidden in

279

the guesthouse. When you and Mr. Walker came out today, the three of us were discussing how to get it out of there safely."

I took a deep breath. So Jackie was playing me. When I told her about the painting being with the police, she knew I was lying. "Mr. Rousseau, I have to ask you a very important question."

"I have no reason to lie to you, Madame. I've told you everything I know. You may ask me anything you like."

"Did you kill Stacey Jordan?"

His face fell. "Ah, my dear Mrs. Sullivan, there is no way I could ever have harmed that sweet girl. No. I am a thief and liar but never a murderer."

Chapter Thirty-Seven

A knock came at the door. "Room service."

"Excuse me, please." Antoine went to answer it.

"Where would you like this, sir?" I could hear a man ask. From where I sat, I couldn't see the waiter or the door.

"On the desk, over there."

Antoine walked back into the room first, followed by a waiter who held a tray topped off with a bottle of wine, two glasses, a corkscrew, and napkins.

I could hear the door slowly closing behind them. As the waiter bent to set the table, something heavy banged against the wall. It took a second for me to realize it was Hank Slater rushing into the room.

The big man tackled Antoine, pushing him forward into the waiter, who went flying toward me. I grabbed my bag and jumped out of the way. Glass shattered, the metal tray went flying, and the wine bottle fell with a thud. The three men rolled around on the floor in a tangle of arms and legs.

"Stop it!" I shouted, trying to understand what was happening. But no one paid any attention to me.

It was obvious Hank was after Antoine.

The waiter managed to pull himself free after a few seconds. Confused, the young man didn't know if he should clean up the glass or retrieve the wine. In the end, he decided against both and ran for the door, slamming it shut behind him. I wondered if he'd call the police or just report it to his supervisor as another out-of-control, drunken guest.

Hank pinned Antoine against the floor. "You grimy snitch. I told Jackie you couldn't be trusted but she wouldn't believe me. All the time going on about what an elegant man you are, what a refined gentleman. Classy my ass!" Then he looked at me. "And you, poking your nose around, you're too old for this crap, ain't ya? No one would have been the wiser if you just butted out and minded your own damn business."

"She called me," Antoine said, nodding toward me, "about the ledger."

I took up the lie. "I did. I called him about Stacey's notes. I don't understand what they mean. I thought maybe Mr. Rousseau would know."

Hank stood up, grabbing Antoine by the wrist and lifting him to a standing position. "You expect me to believe that? I'm not as dumb as you think, lady."

"And just what were you hoping to do, breaking in here like this?" I asked.

"Shut him up—permanently." He jerked Antoine's arm, making the poor man wince in pain. "But since you're here, it looks like I get a two-fer."

"A what?" I asked.

"Two fer the price of one."

He seemed to fill the room as he walked toward me, dragging Antoine along. I backed up, pushing myself against the wall.

Hank reached out, grazing my shoulder with his hand. If it hadn't been for Antoine struggling like he was, Hank would have gotten me on the first try. In spite of his size, he kept being knocked off balance. When Antoine fell to the floor, Hank had to use both hands to pull him up.

Taking advantage of the opportunity, I pulled Nathan's gun out, tossing the bag out of the way. I wondered how many of these little .22 caliber bullets it would take to stop this massive man.

"You're both coming with me now." Yanking Antoine to his feet again, Hank turned back to see me aiming the .22 at his chest.

"We're not going anywhere," I said firmly, never looking away from his eyes. "You're leaving. Get out."

"You're a tough lady, ain't cha?"

He didn't know the half of it. If I had been convinced that he was the killer, I would have shot him right then and there.

He grabbed for the gun, so sure he had everything under control.

I stepped back out of his reach and said, "Look, I don't want to hurt you, Hank. Just let Mr. Rousseau go and—"

"—and you'll call the cops. I know the drill. No, I like my plan better." He grabbed at me again.

And I fired.

The bullet went into the wall.

It was a reflex action that made his arms jerk up, sending Antoine flying into me, knocking me off balance.

Slowly Hank checked his clothing for a sign he'd been shot. When he realized he was okay, he said, "Watch your back, both of you." Then he ran toward the door, crunching glass beneath his shoes, grinding it into the carpet. "This ain't over, Rousseau," he yelled over his shoulder.

When he was gone, Antoine ran to bolt the door.

"You were magnificent, Mrs. Sullivan."

"Yeah, well . . ." I clicked the safety back on the gun. "Pack your bags; we have to get you out of here."

I could see Antoine's hands shaking as he brushed off his suit. "I am afraid you are correct. I've never seen Mr. Slater so angry. What if he should come back or the police have been called?"

He looked frightened at the prospect of being found out and sent to prison. But that was something he'd have to deal with later. I'd come so far with my investigation that I could almost see the finish line. Having Antoine taken in for questioning again would only slow everything down—especially if Bostwick had his way.

"We'll go to my friend Mr. Walker. He'll keep you safe."

"Ahh yes, we met earlier."

While Antoine packed, I called Nathan.

"I'm bringing Antoine along with me to your office. I'll explain later. The police are probably on their way, so I can't talk."

"Are you okay, Kathy?" he asked.

"I'm fine, Nathan."

"And did you find out who killed Stacey?"

"I'll tell you everything when we get there. But I'm starting to think that Hank Slater is the killer."

"Why's that?"

"I'll explain when we get there."

Chapter Thirty~Eight

Nathan had a pot of coffee and a plate of doughnuts laid out for us. I was starving and ever so grateful for his thoughtfulness.

When we walked in the door, he rushed over. "I was so worried."

"I told you I was fine." I smiled at him.

"I know, I know. I just needed to see you for myself."

Antoine stood behind me uncomfortably.

"How're you doing, Mr. Rousseau?" Nathan asked.

"Better now, thanks to Mrs. Sullivan. She is a very brave woman."

"Don't I know," Nathan said. "Come sit down. I'll get you some coffee."

"You are most kind."

While we relaxed, I filled Nathan in on what had happened at the inn. Occasionally, Antoine would make a comment, but not very often. When he left to use the men's room, I quickly told Nathan I was still unsure if Antoine was telling us the truth.

"He knows a hell of a lot more than he's letting on. I've thought that from the start," he said.

I nodded. Before I could say a word, Antoine was back.

We waited until he got settled in his chair. Then Nathan flashed a nice, easy smile.

"So tell me, Mr. Rousseau," he said. "What was your first impression of Jackie Pierce? She's certainly kept tongues wagging in this town with her exploits throughout the years."

Antoine laughed. "I was first struck by her hideous ensemble. But then it has been my experience that wealthy people are most eccentric."

"And all she wanted you to do was keep quiet about her real reason for coming to town?" Nathan asked.

"Oui."

"She never mentioned the Klimt?" I asked.

"Not at first . . ."

"But she did eventually, right?" Nathan asked him.

"Oui. After a while, we did talk about it."

"And you figured that if Stacey found the painting, you'd just . . . keep it?" I asked. "You wouldn't tell Jackie but you would keep the hush money she offered to pay you?"

"Plus his fee from Randolph," Nathan added.

Antoine looked embarrassed but said nothing.

"You never had a conversation with Randolph about his aunt?" I asked. "Did you ever think that she might be crazy and not have the money she promised you?"

"He couldn't ask Randolph anything," Nathan answered for Antoine. "Because if he had, Randolph would have become suspicious, wouldn't he?"

Antoine nodded.

"That day I saw you in front of the gallery, it was after Stacey had been murdered, right?"

"Oui."

"Was it the only time the three of you met?"

"Oh, there were other meetings," Nathan continued. "From the looks of how cozy the three of them were at the guesthouse, I'd say they were becoming very good friends."

"But why would they have to be friends?" I asked Nathan, pretending that I'd forgotten Antoine was even in the room. "If it was all business, they'd have to only meet twice—tops. The first time to make the initial deal and the second time to make payment."

"No," Nathan told me. "Jackie could have just mailed or wired the money to him. No need to meet face to face. They'd want to distance themselves from the crime and each other."

"Which crime?" I asked. "Murder or art theft?"

Nathan shrugged. "I don't know. Maybe both."

Antoine's head swiveled, making him look like he was watching a tennis match.

"If Mr. Rousseau is telling the truth that Stacey was the one who found the painting and was murdered shortly afterwards, I guess both."

"I had nothing to do with Stacey's murder!" Antoine shouted. "I would never hurt that woman. I deal in stolen art, not murder."

"You were using that poor girl from the very start, weren't you?" Nathan asked.

"Knowing she was desperate for money, you figured that if she ever got out of hand, you'd blackmail her. You probably threatened to call the police if she didn't cooperate. And when she actually did find the painting, you . . ."

"Our business would have been concluded. We would have gotten the Klimt out of the country. No one would have been hurt. Please believe me." He looked from Nathan, to me, then back to Nathan. "I was not there, but I'm sure it was an ill-timed . . ."

"Accident. And it screwed up all your plans, right?" I asked him.

The frustrated man nodded. "Sadly, it did."

We gave him a moment. Then after he looked calmer, we started again, right where we'd left off.

"So while they were meeting, over dinner and drinks, what do you suppose the three of them talked about?" I asked Nathan. "It only takes a few hours here and there to discuss the mansion and art. I bet they got personal. That always happens after spending time with people. You exchange anecdotes, jokes, things like that."

"Huh, beats me. But I do know that when

alcohol's involved, tongues get looser. Did you see that bottle of wine at the guesthouse, Kathy? Looked like some excellent stuff there."

We'd worked Antoine up enough so that he wanted to be a part of the conversation. "We talked about the usual," he joined in. "You know how it is. Ourselves, places we had traveled."

"I'm sure you found out more than you ever cared to know about Hank. He does love to talk about himself," I said.

"That he does."

The three of us had to smile.

"And when did he tell you about killing Stacey?" I asked, hoping to shock Antoine with my bluntness.

Antoine didn't look shocked but more upset than anything else. "Never. He never said such a thing."

Nathan leaned back in the desk chair, making it squeak. "So you want us to believe you, Mr. Rousseau, when you say you didn't kill Stacey."

"Definitely."

"Well we have proof that Randolph Pierce couldn't have done it," I said. "If we believe that you didn't kill her, that leaves Hank and Jackie."

"You saw what he was capable of this evening," Antoine said.

"So you're telling us that Hank Slater killed Stacey?" Nathan asked. "And you know this for a fact? Do you have any evidence? And what would his motive have been?"

"It's always been about the paintings," Antoine said.

I jerked forward. "Plural? Are you saying there are more than one at Buckhorn?"

"Well . . . yes and no. I am saying that I was led to believe there could be more."

"Was it Jackie who told you this?" I asked.

"Oui. On more than one occasion."

"Cha-ching! Visions of dollar signs must have been dancing in your head big time." Nathan reached for a doughnut.

"Is that why you're protecting the real killer?" I asked him. "You convinced the police you were innocent early on. So you're in the clear— off their radar. Now all you have to do is finish the restoration, keep your mouth shut . . ."

"And look for more hidden treasure," Nathan finished my sentence.

Antoine looked calm . . . peaceful. He had grown too comfortable with our questioning. What he needed was another good dose of fear to make him tell us everything he knew.

I looked at Nathan. "I was thinking that Mr. Rousseau could stay at your place tonight. Hank might go back out to the inn to . . . you know . . . finish him off."

That did it. Antoine's eyes got wild. "No, it is not safe for me out there!"

"If you're planning to stay in town, you might be better off with a bodyguard," Nathan told him. "Now I got this guy who works for me—"

"Your home would be much better. Please, Mr. Walker. Just for tonight. I beg you."

"Aren't you tired of the danger, Antoine?" I asked him. "You can't finish the job as long as Hank's out there. You can't go home without any compensation for your time. And believe me, I'll tell Randolph not to pay you a cent. I'll tell him how you came here planning to steal from him. I'll even tell him—"

"I give up, Mrs. Sullivan," Antoine said, finally defeated. "I'll tell you everything I know. And if you do exactly as I say, you will catch yourself a killer."

Chapter Thirty-Nine

Later that night, Nathan and I were in the mansion, the scene of the crime. It seemed fitting that this was where the truth should come out.

"I hope she comes," Nathan said.

"She'll come," I assured him. "If she doesn't, it will be like she's admitting she killed Stacey."

We heard someone at the front door.

"Quickly," I said. "Don't let her see you."

Nathan hurried from the room to a hiding place where he could hear everything.

Suddenly, Jackie was in the doorway. She was wearing a long, loose-fitting, dark dress. The subdued outfit was covered with a full-length, green satin coat. Her hair was pulled back away from her face, and I could see the only makeup she'd applied was a coat of red lipstick. The dim lighting exaggerated every wrinkle on her face, adding ten years to her appearance.

"Hello, Jackie. Thank you for agreeing to meet me."

Jackie looked confused. "Well, after you mentioned something about needing my help to get Randolph out of prison, how could I refuse?"

"We've been trying to reconstruct the crime

scene and hoped you might catch something we missed."

"I'll do what I can."

Jackie took a step into the room. The expression on her face as well as her posture seemed to wilt the further she got inside. When she came to a worn chair, she ran her fingers along the leather, caressing the arm with both hands. A slight smile played along her lips but faded instantly. I waited for her to feel comfortable, to walk to the middle of the room.

Antoine had told me the night before when we concocted our plan that over drinks one night, Jackie had shared her darkest secrets with him. She'd told him how her father's verbal abuse had ruined every part of her life. How she'd suffered through her childhood with the tyrant who'd infected not only her self-esteem but her sanity as well. And after one last martini, she told him about the night she'd killed Stacey Jordan.

"That's where Stacey's body was found," I said, pointing to the floor, "but of course, you know that already."

She raised her eyebrows at me and asked, "Do I?"

"Of course you do, Jackie," I said. "You came here that night and found Stacey with the Klimt. You argued. You believe you're the rightful owner of the painting. Isn't that true?"

"That part is true," she said. "After everything my father put me through, I deserve to have the painting."

"And you do have it, don't you?" I asked. "You took it from Stacey that night, after you struck her repeatedly with . . . what? Antoine's stick? Did you have it with you when you came in?"

Jackie looked around to see if anyone else was there.

"I suppose you're wearing some sort of listening device?" she asked. "What do they call it? A wire?"

"I'm not the police, Jackie," I said. "Search me, if you like. It's just you and me here."

"What makes you think I killed Stacey?"

"Well," I said, "for one thing, you've been wearing her bracelet."

She jerked her wrist up and stared at the bracelet, as if it had suddenly burned her.

"I'm not a thief!" she snapped. "Just . . ."

"Just what?" I asked. "A murderer?"

"It wasn't murder," she said. "It was justice. She thought she was going to take my painting. Well, I showed her who it really belonged to."

"By killing her."

She hesitated, then said, "Yes. What else could I do?"

"And was Hank with you?"

"He . . . he had the stick," she said, frowning. "I think I remember him handing it to me.

Anyway, suddenly there it was, in my hand. So I used it."

"And the painting was yours."

"Yes, finally."

"And Hank?"

"He stayed behind to clean up."

"And that's when he took Stacey's bracelet."

"Why?" she said. "Why would he do that?"

"Maybe he thought it was yours, that you dropped it. Or maybe he's not so dumb and gave it to you on purpose, hoping someone would notice and then would figure out you killed Stacey."

That thought seemed to take all the steam out of her.

"I—I don't believe it."

"Why not?" I asked. "With you in jail, Hank could sell the painting and make a tidy profit."

"B-but . . . I killed her for it." Tears began to stream down her cheeks. "Why would he do that to me? Why . . . why do the men in my life . . . treat me . . ." She trailed off and a faraway look came into her eyes. "Daddy?" she said, as if she'd heard her father's voice, and she buried her face in her hands and began to sob. In spite of the fact that I knew she was a killer, it was painful to watch.

As quickly as it had overtaken her, the sobbing stopped and she was calm. Straightening her back, Jackie smoothed her hair, then ran her hands down the front of her dress. And grace-fully she walked out of the room and back down the stairs. Nathan came back into the room as we heard the front door close.

"Well," he said, "that's that. We both heard her confess."

"Yes." Oddly, I didn't feel the least bit triumphant.

Nathan texted Brock to call Bostwick. We both stood at the window watching Jackie walk toward Brock.

Chapter Forty

"Does she think he's Hank?" I wondered aloud.

"Probably."

"Do you think he intentionally took the bracelet off Stacey's wrist?" The idea seemed so ghoulish to me.

"I'm thinking it was on the floor and he just picked it up while he was wiping things off. Maybe he thought it was Jackie's. Or maybe, as you said, he decided to use it to implicate Jackie. When did you think of that?"

"Seconds before I said it. Nathan, you didn't see her face. I think Jackie's got definite . . . problems. I think she heard her father's voice."

"And I'm betting that in spite of her mental problems, Jackie remembers Hank hiding the painting in the guesthouse."

"We'll soon find out."

It was dark outside on the lawn. All the lights had been shut off earlier. As we slowly opened the door, we could hear Jackie.

"I did it again," she told Brock. "Go fix it like you did before. Make everything right, sweetheart. If you love me, you'll help me."

Brock had been briefed and knew what to expect. "I'll fix it, don't worry," he told her.

But even in her confusion, Jackie knew the

man standing in front of her was an imposter. "Where's Hank?" she screamed at the top of her lungs. "Hank! Are you out here?"

Two police cars were pulling up as we walked outside. Jackie looked bewildered as the red and blue lights illuminated her face.

"Now if Antoine did as he promised and called Hank to come to the mansion, all the loose ends will be tied up," I said. "I don't like loose ends."

As Jackie was being gently led to one of the police cars, Hank casually walked from the direction of the guesthouse. His expression changed immediately when he saw what was happening. And when he saw me standing there next to Nathan, he started to run. But in order to get to his car, he had to go through the small crowd, which he did without hesitation. For a moment, I thought he was going to plow right into Jackie. Brock must have thought so, too, because he tackled Hank before he could harm the small woman.

Bostwick looked on amused as the two large men wrestled across the lawn. But when he handcuffed Jackie, his humor changed to pity.

When Brock stood Hank up, two officers came over and handcuffed him, too.

"You got the wrong guy, and when I get done with you, you'll be back to writing parking tickets. Check that fancy stick of his. It'll have that girl's blood all over it. You need someone like me to tell you it's the murder weapon? She may have used it, but Frenchie was always leaving it behind. You might have me now, but I'll testify against them and I'll walk."

"Hank's not as smart as he thinks," I said to Nathan. "He doesn't realize that between Antoine's alibi and polygraph results, he's in the clear on the murder."

"It's obvious he tried to frame Antoine by giving him back his walking stick. And the whole time, the clueless Frenchman was carrying it around. Well I guess there's no need for us to go to the police station, is there?"

"No, but before we leave I have to go tell Bostwick to pick up the walking stick from Antoine."

Chapter Forty-One

"Mother! Wake up! You have to see this!"

I hurried out to the kitchen. Chloe and Cam stopped eating their breakfast when they saw me.

"They're talking about you on TV, Grammy," Cam said.

"OMG! Jennifer's gonna be über jealous. All her grandmother does is make quilts." Chloe giggled.

While I enjoyed having their attention, I looked to Lizzie to help me understand what was happening.

"It's all over the news," Lizzie pointed to the television.

Along the bottom of the screen was a red banner with yellow letters, announcing *BREAKING NEWS*. A serious-looking man read from a paper he held with both hands. "Last night, socialite and prominent citizen, Jacqueline Bannister-Pierce, was arrested for the murder of Stacey Jordan. The arrest came about after police were tipped off by a private investigator, former chief of police, Katherine Sullivan."

Cam looked up at me. "That's you, Grammy!"

"It wasn't just me. Nathan and Brock were there, too." I told them.

"Miss Jordan had been employed by Randolph Pierce, nephew of the accused, to assist with renovations at Buckhorn manor. Ownership of the mansion is scheduled to be transferred to the state of Minnesota on the centennial of its groundbreaking, which is later this year. Mrs. Bannister-Pierce, seventy-two, has been struggling with mental health problems for years. She is scheduled to be examined by a court-appointed psychiatrist who will determine if she is fit to stand trial. At this time, she is being held at the county jail. Her longtime companion, Henry Slater, forty-five, was also arrested. Mr. Slater allegedly tampered with evidence at the crime scene, interfering with the police investigation. If you're interested in learning more about the history of the Pierce family, and Buckhorn mansion, go to our website. Once again, Jacqueline Bannister-Pierce has been arrested for murder."

An anchorwoman sitting next to her male counterpart came into the shot. "I know you've only been living in Edina for a few months, Bill, but were you aware of the rumors surrounding Buckhorn?"

"Not at first, Sandy. But after researching the history of the estate, I was surprised to learn that there was supposedly a priceless painting hidden inside."

"Well apparently those rumors were true.

Authorities claim that an original Klimt was the motive for the murder."

"And where is it now?" he asked her.

"Police are still searching but we'll keep you updated." Big smile. "And now for your local weather."

"I have to call Nathan," I said and rushed to my room to dress.

"I told Rousseau he'd be safe at the inn. Brock even went out to check on him after leaving the mansion last night." Nathan steered toward Lake Minnetonka.

"And he was there all safe and sound?" I asked.

"Sure was. Brock said they even had a beer together. He assured Rousseau that Bostwick had arrested Hank and Jacqueline."

"That should have made him feel better."

"Then why did he skip town?" Nathan asked.

"Let me try something." I dug out my cell phone and called the station. The administrative aide, Bobby Hill, answered. He had worked for me near the end of my time there.

"There's a team out at the property right now, Mrs. Sullivan. They did a thorough search of the mansion right after the murder, but today Chief Bostwick told 'em to turn that guest-house upside down. They're not to come back without that painting."

"So as far as you know, it hasn't been found yet?"

"That's what I'm hearin'."

"Thanks, Bobby."

"Sure, Chief."

I almost hung up, then said, "Bobby, wait!"

"Yeah, Chief?"

"Did they find Rousseau's walking stick in his room?"

"They did," Bobby said. "The Chief had it sent to forensics."

Hank said it was the murder weapon but that didn't make it legally so. Bostwick was going to have to confirm that with tests.

"Okay, Bobby. I might see you later. I'll probably come in and see the Chief."

"Right," he said and hung up.

I told Nathan what I knew.

"Rousseau swore up and down that Hank hid the painting out there."

"I know, but come on, Nathan, the guy's a con man."

"Yeah. The way they get you is by throwing in a few lies with most of the truth."

"How long have you been trying to call him?" I asked.

"Since six this morning. He swore that once Hank and Jackie were arrested, he'd give a statement to Bostwick."

"He's probably afraid we'd turn him in for his connection to the black market. That ledger would likely implicate him."

"It probably would."

"I've got to give it to Bostwick."

"If you do, he'll know you took it from Stacey's apartment. The chain of evidence will be broken. It'll be inadmissible, Kathy."

I thought about that for a moment.

"Who's at your office now?"

"E.T."

"And the ledger's in a safe place?"

"Locked up tight."

"It's going to implicate Stacey and Antoine, for sure. Nathan, can you have Brock go back to Stacey's and return the book to its hiding place?"

"So that Bostwick can find it there? Good thinking. I'll call him."

He took out his cell phone and made a quick call, then hung up.

"Can he do it?"

"He said for you, anything."

"He's a big sweetie."

"I just thought of something else, though."

"What?"

"The restoration is still an ongoing project. Antoine hasn't gotten paid yet. He'll definitely want that money before he leaves town."

"But he's said over and over that the most important thing to him is his reputation. Don't you think he's afraid that Hank or Jackie will mention his involvement to the police?"

"So you do think he's skipped out on us?" Nathan asked.

"Looks that way. But let's check the inn, just to be sure."

"Sorry, Mrs. Sullivan," the desk clerk said. "Mr. Rousseau checked out last night."

"Can you tell me what time that would have been?"

"Not exactly but the night guy found Mr. Rousseau's room key on the desk when he started his shift at midnight."

"Is there anyone who might have seen him leaving?"

"Wait a minute. I have an idea." The clerk waved to a maid who was coming out of a room right off the lobby. "Celia!" When the maid stopped, the clerk walked over to talk with her.

Nathan and I waited until they were finished.

When they were done, the clerk returned and the maid walked back down the hall.

"She says that when she went to turn down his bed at nine last night, he wasn't there. That's the best we can do."

"Did he leave anything behind?" I asked.

"No. In fact, his room was so clean that she joked we should hire him to work here."

"Thanks so much."

Nathan handed her one of his cards. "If you see Mr. Rousseau, you can reach us here."

"I'll remember that."

As we walked back to the car, Nathan and I discussed if we should spend any more time trying to find Antoine Rousseau. My job was finished; I'd proven that Randolph Pierce was not a murderer and handed the real killer to the police to boot. I'd done everything I'd set out to do and more. Now it was up to the cops to make a case against Jackie and Hank and make it stick.

"So do you think Rousseau got away with the painting?" Nathan wondered.

"I know I shouldn't care, but it's driving me crazy not knowing," I said.

"If he did," Nathan said, "he wouldn't worry about collecting his money from Pierce."

I sighed. "I'd like to be done with this, but I know I'll have to go see Bostwick later."

"You want me to come with you?"

"No, I'll be fine," I assured him. "You and Dean don't mix well."

"And you do?"

Chapter Forty-Two

When we walked in, E.T. was rearranging the desks in the main room.

Nathan looked amused. "What are you doing?"

"I've been wanting to do this for a long time," E.T. told him, rolling a chair closer to the window. "The feng shui in here is all messed up. Believe me, Boss, once I get the harmony flowing again, you'll feel the difference."

"You knew the man was like this when you hired him," I said, watching in amusement. "What can it hurt to jazz up the harmony in here?"

"Is Brock on his way to Minneapolis?" Nathan asked E.T.

"Yep, with the ledger," E.T. said.

Nathan shook his head again at the feng shui and walked into his office. E.T. was oblivious to much except his project. I followed Nathan. He sat behind his desk with a heavy sigh.

"Can I borrow your car?"

Nathan stood up and reached in his pocket. "I have a lot of work to catch up on here. When will you be back?" he asked, tossing the keys to me.

Making a successful catch, I opened my mouth in exaggerated surprise. "You're letting me go alone without a single word of caution or a list of instructions?"

He stood up and folded his arms across his chest. "The bad guys are behind bars, Rousseau is gone, and hey, you're a big girl . . ."

"And I can take care of myself. Admit it. Come on . . . say it."

"You can take care of yourself. Happy?"

"I'll be even happier after I tie up this loose end."

"And return my car!"

"You're such a nag."

I tried not looking too smug as I sat across from Dean Bostwick, but it was very difficult.

"I'm surprised to see you here. Isn't your PI job all finished?" He leaned back in his chair and smiled at me. He was being very cordial, and I decided to play it the same way.

"What can I do for you?" he asked.

"I was wondering if you got back the forensics report on Antoine's walking stick?"

Bostwick looked sheepish. "Good catch on that. No, I don't have it back yet, but Hank assured us it was the murder weapon. I think it'll check out."

"What about Antoine?"

"He may have left town, but if he hasn't, I've put him on the no-fly list. But I'm thinking that he might be waiting until Pierce is released to settle up with him. Also, if he has the painting, he has to figure out how to get it out of the country. He can't just waltz onto a plane holding a priceless painting under his arm."

I laughed. "You got that right. And how's Jackie?"

"She hasn't quite come all the way back from around the bend, yet," he admitted. "She did, however, confess to killing her brother, Leland, all those years ago."

"She drowned her own brother?" I couldn't believe it.

Bostwick nodded. "Seemed he was Daddy's favorite."

"Poor Jackie."

"The woman's a murderer, Katherine," Bostwick said. "I have no sympathy for her. In fact, we're reexamining the conditions under which Marshall Senior died. Who knows?"

"Wow! At least she can't kill anyone else."

"So did you just drop by to check up on the murder weapon?"

"No. I really stopped by to bring you a little . . . present, Dean."

"It's all in a day's work. There's no need to thank me for anything."

"There's a ledger I think you might be interested in."

"What's in it?"

"I think it's a list of people who have illegally

purchased stolen art from Stacey and Antoine Rousseau."

His eyes popped and he looked like he'd just won the lottery. "How do you know? Where did you get this?"

"Oh, I can't reveal my source, Dean." I stood to leave.

"Where's this book—you know, if you touched it, or moved it, it'll be inadmissible."

"I think if you send somebody to Stacey's Minneapolis apartment tomorrow, they'll find it in the kitchen, on a shelf with a bunch of cookbooks."

"Katherine . . ."

I stopped at the door and turned to look at him, making my face as innocent as possible.

He threw his hands in the air and just said, "Thanks for the tip."

Chapter Forty~Three

I stopped to sit on a bench outside the police station and bask in the warm sunlight and my glory. They both felt wonderful. Then I called Lizzie's office number.

"Oh hey, Mrs. Sullivan," her assistant Josh said. "Mrs. Farina's with her client, Mr. Pierce, at the jail. Lots of paperwork to fill out before he can walk out of there. But she said to meet her at the gallery around two."

"I imagine she's very happy today."

"I'd say she's more relieved than anything else. She's had a hard time of it. Good thing you were here to help her."

"Thanks, Josh. Tell her I'll see her later."

"Will do. Have a nice day."

"It can't get much nicer."

Squeezing Nathan's car into a parking space, I could see a crowd of people inside the Pierce Gallery. It looked like several women were holding champagne glasses and one man was laughing uncontrollably, but I couldn't see Randolph or Lizzie.

As I entered the building, I was overwhelmed with the joyful scene. An old Elton John song played through the speakers, red and gold metallic balloons clung to the ceiling, and a waiter walked by with a tray of appetizers. When I waved him off, he told me that champagne was being served in the back of the room.

Walking the perimeter of the room, I sipped champagne and planned to stay another ten minutes before leaving. After years of hearing Lizzie complain about Dandy Randy, listening to Sully tell me all the trouble the Pierce boy was constantly getting into, I was glad to see he had enough friends to fill the gallery. But then I reminded myself that Randolph Pierce was a grown man now. He was a business owner and, from the looks of it, a respected and well-liked member of the community. Not the troubled rich kid I remembered.

"There you are!" Randolph stood in front of me. "Lizzie was afraid you wouldn't come."

"Why is that?" I asked.

"Come on, Mrs. Sullivan. We all know I'm not your favorite person."

"I don't really know you, Randolph."

"Well in spite of what you think of me, I thank you for helping me clear my name. And I bet for a while that maybe . . . just maybe . . . you might have thought I had murdered Stacey, didn't you?"

"Well . . ."

"I don't blame you, Mrs. Sullivan. I was a real

313

jerk for a lot of years. But you and Mr. Sullivan were always fair with me."

I was starting to warm up to him. "Well it looks like you turned out okay."

"Almost getting arrested for murder? I don't know how good that is but at least it's over. I'm just afraid this will follow me forever. Once something gets put out there, it never goes away. And I have plans, things I want to do with my life, which could be difficult if people think I'm capable of murder."

"Do you want some motherly advice?"

"From you . . . always." He started to put his arm around me but realized it was too soon for such an affectionate gesture.

"People are always going to think what they want to think. Some won't like you for no good reason at all. It might be for something silly like the way you comb your hair. Others will hate you on sight. Maybe you remind them of a bully who taunted them in school."

His smile drooped. "So you're telling me to not even try because it doesn't matter?"

"If trying is what you want to do, then by all means try to change public opinion. But what I'm saying is don't waste your precious time worrying about things you can't change—that's all. Do what makes you happy but never hurt anyone along the way." I patted his shoulder. "And I'll tell you a secret."

"Which is?"

"We're all blessed with short memories. Once a new scandal hits, some teen idol gets picked up for shoplifting or getting into a fight at a dance club, you'll be old news."

"But Lizzie told me you gave her a lecture a few days ago about how important her reputation was. How people don't forget and hold grudges."

He'd caught me. "Well, she's my daughter. When you have children, you'll learn that you have to kind of customize your advice, depending on the child and situation."

"Oh, I get it. Different strokes for different folks."

"Exactly."

When we started laughing, it was hard to stop.

"There you are!" Lizzie hugged me. "Isn't it wonderful? Everything worked out perfectly. I'm so proud of you, Mother. Isn't she wonderful?" she asked Randolph.

"Katherine Sullivan is an amazing woman." Randolph held up his crystal champagne flute and then took a drink.

"Houdini was amazing. A man walking on the moon, now that's really amazing. But me? No." Where had I been the day that word had been reduced to it basest form? And why was it that everyone now used it when describing anything barely acceptable?

"Okay then, how about . . . wonderful?" Randy asked.

"Much better."

While the three of us continued talking, people kept arriving for the celebration and I started feeling claustrophobic. I was nibbling on a cracker spread with brie when Nathan walked through the door. I watched him study the room and the people in it, but he didn't see me.

Shoving the rest of the cracker in my mouth, I grabbed another glass of champagne and pushed through the crowd.

He was looking thoughtfully at a canvas splattered with cobalt blue and bright yellow. I walked up behind him and tapped his shoulder.

As he turned around, I asked, "Champagne, sir?"

"Don't mind if I do." He took the glass, never giving me the satisfaction of showing one bit of surprise at seeing me there.

"What are you doing here?" I asked.

"Looking for you . . . and my car."

"I was going to bring it back right after I left here. I'd never leave you stranded."

"I know, Kathy, I was just playing with you. I used E.T.'s van. He's still wrestling with furniture. When I left, he was moving pictures around. No, I got a call from DeYoung. Sounds like you got in the last word with ol' Bostwick. You're big news."

"But how did you know I'd be here?"

"That took some real detective work." He winked. "Lizzie called and invited me."

"Well I'm glad you're here."

"If you've had enough pats on the back, the crew wants to say good-bye. How much longer do you think you'll be?"

"I'm ready to leave this party now."

"Just let me go say hi to that lovely daughter of yours, and Pierce of course, then we'll get outta here."

Chapter Forty-Four

They were all there when we got to the office, including Brock, who was back from his errand in Minneapolis. A desk had been pushed into the middle of the room and the crew was seated around it. Two pizzas were the centerpiece.

"Here she is, the woman of the hour," Nathan said as he took my jacket.

The four of them stood up and clapped.

"Come on, you guys, this was a joint effort." I applauded them.

Brock pushed a chair toward me. "Have a seat, Katherine."

"And hurry. These jerks wouldn't let me eat a bite until you got here," Rosie said.

Polly passed around paper plates. "What would you like to drink, Kate?"

"Soda's fine."

She handed me a can of Coke.

E.T. looked at the food with a concerned frown. "The one on the left is vegetarian, right?" he asked.

"You can see it is," Brock told him, annoyed. "Stop fussing and just eat, will ya?"

Nathan took a slice, grabbed a napkin, and started his little speech. "I thought we'd take some time to celebrate the fine work all of us have done the past few days. Good job, every-one. Thanks to your talents, the real killer's in jail and Pierce is free. I want you all to know how much I appreciate everything."

"And?" E.T. asked.

"Oh yeah, and we're also here to say good-bye to Kathy."

The five of them raised their pizza in a salute.

"You've all been great. But maybe this cele-bration is premature. There's still a trial and . . ."

"What's wrong?" Rosie asked.

"I don't mean to be a wet blanket but a few things have been bothering me."

"Stop being so hard on yourself, Katie," Rosie said. "Everything turned out great and every-one's happy. That's all she wrote; there ain't no more."

"I agree," E.T. said. "All's well that ends well."

But the detail-minded Polly asked, "What's the problem?"

I addressed my concerns to her. "The murder weapon. I knew it was shaped like a globe, that it was made of metal. Antoine's stick was obvious. I should have let Nathan go back to the guesthouse that day and grab it."

"And then what?" he asked. "We would've taken it to Nylander to be tested. There goes two or three days. If it turned out to be the murder weapon, then what? Any one of those three, Slater, Jackie, or Rousseau, could have used it.

But more than likely it would have been wiped clean, like the crime scene, and we would have been spinning our wheels."

"But I could have . . . I should have . . ."

"Hey, you spotted it in the first place, which is more than I did. And when Hank started flapping his gums last night, you knew you'd been right. I guess you'll have to be satisfied with that," Nathan said.

I knew he was right but still . . .

"So what else? You said 'things.' What other thing is bothering you?" Polly wanted to know.

"That stupid bracelet. I just can't believe Jackie was dumb enough to flaunt it, knowing that someone might realize it had belonged to Stacey."

"Antoine told us Hank picked it up while he was cleaning the murder scene," Nathan told the others.

" 'Picked it up.' That's the way he said it?" E.T. asked. "Which means it was lying there, in a separate area, away from the body. So why wouldn't he think it belonged to Mrs. Pierce?"

"You know, sometimes the answer is right in front of your face," I said, relieved.

"So that's it, now?" Rosie asked. "You're okay?"

"I'm good."

It was great being there with that odd bunch. They all had so many great stories to tell and I listened to them for hours. It was well past ten by the time we'd run out of steam.

I said my good-byes, promising to see them all next time I was in town, extending an invitation for them to come visit me. Nathan asked, several times, that I call when I got home so he'd know I was safe.

I wanted to tell him how much I'd miss him. But with everyone there—well—it was difficult. And I wanted to give him a real kiss good-bye, but . . .

Maybe next time.

Chapter Forty-Five

As we sat around the dinner table the next evening, I gave Chloe back her phone. She didn't seem all that excited to see it.

"Thanks, Grandma." She gave a quick smile and went back to eating.

"Now you can stop being angry."

That's what got her. "I wasn't angry. Mom, was I angry?" Not giving any of us a chance to contradict her, she continued talking. "I just don't like people up in my face, telling me what to do."

"But, Chloe, you're only thirteen."

Lizzie looked at me like I'd just walked into a minefield.

"Thirteen-year-old girls aren't like they were when you were young, Grandma. Back in the olden days, it was all, you can't be a doctor, you have to be a nurse or a teacher. Go have babies. But now it's girl power."

I had to admire her moxie. But still, I wanted to point out that I had commanded the respect of squads of policemen. I was a powerful . . . aww, she wouldn't get it. Not when her heroes were singers and models.

Cam had been listening, quietly eating his

chicken, while the conversation circled around him. "So what's new with you?" I asked. "What new masterpieces are you working on?"

"What happened to that painting? The . . . Klimt?" When he asked, I was surprised that he had been absorbing all the facts of the case. But why wouldn't he? Lizzie and I had talked about it, and the news was full of it now that everything was done with.

"I got word a little while ago that they caught Antoine trying to leave with the painting. The case is really closed, now."

"I was wondering, Grammy . . ."

"What, Cam?"

"Do you think me and you could go together, to that mansion, and do some art before you leave?"

"I think it can be arranged, sweetie."

Spring had catapulted into summer overnight, and the temperature was eighty as Cam and I set up our easels on the grounds in front of the Pierce estate. He'd wanted to sketch the intricate brickwork and stained glass patterns as seen from the outside. I adjusted my wide-brimmed hat and looked over at Cam, who was wearing a Minnesota Twins cap. I'd swabbed his face with sunscreen against his protests.

It took me a while to get everything set up, squeeze a dab of paint on the palette, mix it with

a little brown, but Cam started drawing immediately. And I waited, knowing the best part of
the day was going to be our private conversation.

"Did I ever tell you about your art project?
You know, the one you did with the blocks? Did
you know it helped me solve the case?"

"Yeah, you said it reminded you of that lady's
bracelet."

"Right."

"But it really wasn't her bracelet, was it? The
old one, I mean. It belonged to Miss Jordan,
right?"

"That it did."

"So how did she get it, then?"

"She got it by mistake." I explained the chain
of events to him.

Cam giggled. "And her dumb boyfriend just
went along with her. That's what guys do when a
girl likes them. They just do anything to make
her smile."

"Do you have girlfriend?"

"Kinda."

"What does that mean?" I asked.

"It means she doesn't know she's my girlfriend."

"Well, be sure to tell her," I said, squinting to
get the color of the driveway just right.

"Maybe." Cam's fingers never took a break.
From the time he'd set up, he'd been sketching

and talking, quite able to do both comfortably. "So when are you coming back?"

"Oh, I don't know. But you and your mom and Chloe could come out to visit me. There's so much to inspire you in the Southwest. You'd love all the colors. Maybe you'd even start working in oils or—"

"I like it here."

"Well . . . maybe someday."

We worked in silence for more than an hour. Other than the birds that chirped and flew around us and an occasional squirrel dashing up a tree, we were all alone out there.

I took out a bottle of water and offered it to Cam. He drank a little and handed it back to me. I took a sip. The sun was moving slowly, taking our shade away. I was thinking that another twenty minutes should do it before we'd either have to move or leave.

"Why do they sometimes call this place the Pierce estate and then the estate and then Buckhorn manor?" Cam asked. "And what's a Buckhorn anyway? Is that someone's name?"

"Well, all those names refer to this place. Some people remember when the Pierce family lived here, like I do. They grew up thinking of it that way. Estate just means a big fancy house with lots of land around it. And Buckhorn, now that's interesting. It's a poisonous plant. See those shrubs over there?" I pointed with my brush.

"Those are buckhorns. People used them to make paint, but that was a long time ago."

"Huh."

"So how you doing?" I asked. "Ready to go?"

"Can we stop for ice cream on the way home?"

"Anything for my fellow artist. Let me see what you got there."

The façade of the mansion had been captured like a photograph. I had to look from the real thing to the sketch pad to compare a cracked brick, the pineapple doorknocker. "I'm so impressed, Cam."

He took a few steps to come closer and look over my shoulder. "Yours is nice, Grammy." After studying my watercolor, he asked, "Can I borrow your brush?"

"Sure." I handed it to him.

He took the brush that had been dipped in green, and in broad strokes, he waved it across his sketch. I didn't try to stop him, I was too fascinated.

When he was finished, he'd made Buckhorn look more like a magic castle instead of the brick and glass structure I was trying to capture.

"That's better," he said, satisfied.

I don't know how he managed it, but it was better. Seeing what he had done, I made a promise to myself. I'd stop painting landscapes for a while and concentrate more—no, I wouldn't concentrate at all next time. That was the trick. I'd just paint from my heart the way he did.

Center Point Large Print

600 Brooks Road / PO Box 1
Thorndike, ME 04986-0001 USA

(207) 568-3717

US & Canada:
1 800 929-9108
www.centerpointlargeprint.com